CLIFFS

OLIVIER ADAM

CLIFFS

Translated from the French
by Sue Rose

PUSHKIN PRESS
LONDON

For Florian

English translation © Sue Rose 2007

First published in French as
Falaises © Editions de l'Olivier 2005

This edition first published in 2007 by

Pushkin Press
12 Chester Terrace
London N1 4ND

British Library Cataloguing in Publication Data:
A catalogue record for this book is available
from the British Library

ISBN (13) 978 1 901285 75 8
ISBN (10) 1 901285 75 8

All rights reserved. No part of this publication may be
reproduced, stored in a retrieval system or transmitted in
any form or by any means, electronic, mechanical,
photocopying, recording or otherwise,
without prior permission in writing from
Pushkin Press

Cover © Beatrice Caracciolo Courtesy of the Artist

Frontispiece: Olivier Adam 2006
© Bruno Garcin Gasser

Set in Monotype Baskerville
and printed in United Kingdom
by TJ International

It is my childhood and I have no other
  HENRI CALET

For Karine

I

IN THE SAND

Here the night is deep and dark as the world. On the other side of the plate-glass windows, cut off from the outside and the cliffs, shielded from the sound of the sea and the company of birds, Claire is sleeping and who knows where we're headed. Chloé lies in her arms, slight and peaceful against her chest. I light candles in the dark. My hand dips into the clear plastic bag and I take out small round aluminium cups filled with white wax. I strike a match. It's twenty years since my mother died. Twenty years to the day.

The cliffs cut into the cloth of the sky. I see ghosts there, bodies falling through the light. I turn round and the glass reflects my gaunt face, my drawn features, prematurely old. Claire opens her eyes for a second, Chloé puts her thumb in her mouth, and snuggles up against her back. I light a cigarette and its incandescent tip forms a red circle, a bright point of light amid the black and white. Two loungers face each other on the balcony where I keep vigil above the beach. I lie down on one. A blanket protects me from the intensifying cold. I gaze west, unseeing.

I'm thirty-one and my life is just beginning. I don't have a childhood and, from now on, any childhood will do. My mother is dead and everyone I cared about has gone. Life has wiped me clean, like the empty table at which Claire and I are sitting and at which Chloé has pulled up a chair, a sweet smile playing at the corners of her mouth.

I'm thirty-one and this is how my life is beginning, adrift in the darkness by the sea. Behind me, scarcely more tangible than shadows, less substantial than a wisp of smoke, Claire and Chloé watch me, the little girl in the woman's arms, both motionless in the quiet hotel room. Claire smiles at me then goes back to sleep, and their breathing merges.

Here the night is deep and dark with a world of people. My mother wanders the moor, like a sleepwalking wraith. Antoine and Nicolas, Lorette and the others dance round the flames, their eyes closed and their faces upturned. Léa stands on the edge, balanced on tiptoe as if on a high-wire, a hair's breadth from the drop, funambulist, tightrope-walker.

I WAS ELEVEN when my mother died. Three days earlier, she came out of the hospital and everything was splashed with light. She had spent the last six months in there and we hadn't been allowed to see her. The ornamental lake, the straight line of benches, the tall birch trembling near the building, the fir in the middle of the lawn, the cherry trees in blossom, I remember it all, if hazily.

We were waiting for her in the car, my father at the wheel of his grey Ford Granada, my brother and I curled up against each other, quiet in the back. The perforated leatherette stuck to our thighs, marked our damp skin. My father was drumming his fingertips against the dashboard, fiddling with the Paris Saint-Germain football pennant hanging from the rear-view mirror, and every now and then he turned round and ordered us to behave ourselves, although we were barely breathing. Antoine nodded and I copied him. Then I closed my eyes and the sun bit into my cheek.

Suddenly my father got out of the car, I sat up straight and the sunlight was dazzling. I closed my eyes again then opened them and there she was in the distance. She was walking towards us, emotionless and transparent, on the other side of the iron gates. Looking pale and wearing a long red coat, her right arm in a sling and one hand in bandages, she seemed not to see us. She walked slowly towards us, right in the middle of the wide path, small and alone in the motionless park. It was as if everything, trees and fountains, had been turned to stone, as if time had come to a halt in endless winter. When she saw my father, she didn't show the slightest reaction. They kissed half-heartedly, their lips barely brushing or perhaps they didn't even touch. He took hold of her suitcase. She lit a cigarette. She had lost weight and her face was clouded behind the whorls of smoke. Antoine squeezed my wrist and I listened to his convulsive breathing. We stared at her, unable to move. It was unbearably hot inside the car. My brother's hair was plastered against his forehead in dark strands. She climbed in without kissing us. For a long while, she didn't move; her eyes were fixed on the road, the far-off fields, or perhaps she closed them. Then she turned round with the faintest of smiles. I held my breath, my heart wrung like an old sponge. I waited for her lips to form a word, but nothing emerged. She turned back and my father started the car. She didn't say anything when he turned onto the motorway.

We drove in silence for miles. Unable to take our eyes off the back of our mother's neck, we tracked her slightest movement, the way she tucked her hair behind her ears, the way her shoulders lifted slightly as she breathed in. Our faces unwavering in the hum of the motorway, the blurred motion of the passing cars, we waited hearts racing for her to turn round, look at us affectionately, blow us a kiss. The engine noise swamped everything. In the end I fell asleep against my brother, our faces touching. My father turned on the heater and the air became warm and nauseating.

Some time later, the car drew to a halt. Darkness had just fallen. The service station was ugly and livid in the headlights. There was a light drizzle, you could barely feel it, in your hair, on your cheeks. It looked like a very fine curtain in the streetlights, bubbles in a bottle of sparkling water. My father went to get a coffee. In the car park he stretched and, to look at him, who would have thought he was going through such a critical time, that he'd just been reunited with his wife who'd spent months in a psychiatric clinic. He could just as easily have been our driver, and that's what he really was, at the wheel of his taxi. Leaning back against the car, my mother smoked a cigarette; Antoine rubbed his eyes and yawned. She stubbed out her butt looking up at the sky, gave a sigh I didn't understand, and grabbed my hand. I took hold of my brother's hand. We filed into the shop among shelves of crisps, sweets, biscuits. She swept up products as if at random, indiscriminately picking out packets of cakes and chewing gum, sugary drinks. She stopped by a display stand and spun it round. Cheap jewellery whirled in the harsh light. The loudspeakers were playing a song by Michel Delpech, *Les Divorcés*; I don't know why I remember such a precise detail when I've forgotten so many important things. We each chose a wristband, a brown leather wristband printed with our name. I still have mine. I have no idea why she wanted to buy us that. To have our names stamped on our wrists. I had the vague feeling that we should have put a wristband, even a collar, on her so that we would never lose her again.

My father finished his coffee and we walked back to the car. In only a few minutes the interior had chilled and the leatherette felt like an ice shelf beneath our half-bare legs. For the rest of the journey, mum sat in the back, between the two of us, as if she at last felt capable of it, as if she'd needed time to adapt before she could manage it. We slept with our heads on her lap, or pretended to. The perfume of her dress mingled with the smell of the heater and sweat. I felt her fingers on my forehead or in my hair. And my brother's cheek against mine, our damp skin and his breathing merging with the engine noise. From time to time, mum leant over and kissed me. I kept my eyes shut, I held my breath, content under her regained kisses, in the dark of the car, the muffled murmur of the radio.

We arrived at about ten o'clock in the evening. The restaurants were shutting up and the promenade was deserted. Girls in aprons were stacking chairs, placing them upside down on washed tables. Cooks were smoking beside dustbins. Everything was filled with the booming of the waves and, at that time, the white cliffs weren't brightly outlined against the darkness of the sky. I've stayed in Étretat, for a few hours or longer, many times since that day, twenty years ago now. It's impossible to say exactly when they started illuminating the cliffs, what year those immense floodlights were put there. All I know is that since then, whenever I come here, I always take the same room at the Hôtel des Corsaires, room 103, and that I spend most of my nights on the balcony, lying on a plastic lounger, wrapped up warmly in blankets, gazing at the unreal sight of the evenly striated, luminous rocks plunging straight down into complete darkness. On those nights, I smoke until all the lights go out and the world is suddenly returned to the sea, reduced to the roar of the surf, the tumbled shingle. This is the third time Claire has come with me, the first since Chloé was born. I don't know if all this makes any sense to her, the time I spend staring at that chalky mass with its gaunt peak, the endless wheeling of the birds in front of it, either on this narrow balcony or, earlier in the day, sitting on the beach, tirelessly letting smooth pebbles slip through my fingers.

WHEN SHE REALISED we were driving towards Étretat, that we'd be spending the night there, even a few days if all went well, my mother had no particular reaction. All the same I'd watched for a smile, a gleam in her eyes; the recollection of her hand in her own mother's hand, she was eight, nine or ten and they were quietly walking up and down the spit of shingle overlooked by the cliffs. In the evening after the beach, they drove to Fécamp, where they stayed with a female friend. I keep three photos in my wallet in which my mother is a skinny girl smiling in a pale swimsuit, shallow waves lapping round her feet. In one, a short woman in a flowery blouse is smoking a cigarette near some long wooden slides. It's a real effort for me to recognise my grandmother in this photo. My first memory dates back to her death, or thereabouts. That's the thing: I only remember her after her death, like an imprint, a cavity. The memory of a memory. I don't remember her square face, her rustic ways, her thick glasses, her dyed, curly hair that she protected from the rain with a triangle of clear plastic, her pious gestures, the murmured prayers on her lips, the worried kindness in her eyes, the care she took of her family, her concern. Even less, my grief at her death. All I recall is an all-encompassing, heady affection, the vague recollection of my head against her bosom, the tracks left by her steady gaze on my skin. And the things Antoine told me about her, in the alcohol-fuelled dark, during stopovers that were always too short. He was sometimes swamped by too many tears, incomprehensible words, a mishmash of unfinished sentences encapsulating our childhood and everything I'd forgotten about it, our mother's death, Laetitia's body, and the rifle Nicolas put in his mouth when he was sixteen. Then, like a balm, my grandmother always materialised, her signs of the cross and her kisses on our foreheads, the multicoloured blankets and cushions she knitted, a large blue flower in the middle of the orange, the bottles she covered with wool and transformed into dogs, cats or little people, the balcony of her flat where we leant over trees, squirrels, tiny passers-by, the photos of her husband on the sideboard with its row of horrible doilies and crude imitation crystal, her tremulous gaze, sustained by bottomless kindness, piety, compassion, mercy, our ball games in the park, her knitted brows as she checked our homework that always baffled her, our footsteps in the forest hardened by winter, the coffin he'd seen disappear into the hole when I wasn't there, her voice reading us stories in the half-light of a bedroom, the small black Bible tattered by repeated reading, the crucifix we sometimes took down from above her bed, standing straight reaching up, our hands jostling round the edges, while she said she was just 'resting' and we knew she had a terminal illness that she knew nothing about (she might also have been pretending not to know), then she'd talk and talk, an incredible light deep in her eyes (which I now tell myself came from the promise of reaching heaven at last), about summers to come, games in the grass, tennis, pétanque and croquet, amongst the daisies or in the shade of an elm, and her plans for showing us the region of high cliffs and wheeling birds. We'd nod with forced smiles that didn't fool anyone. I was eight when she died, Antoine was ten and that's the year my memories begin. My earliest image is centred around her, but she isn't in it, she's already dead and buried. My first memory is a stolen moment, an interruption. Abandoning my homework, sheets of paper and notebooks spread out beneath the lamp on the small light wood desk against the radiator (through the window, you could make out a mask on the orange tiled roof of the millstone house opposite, a face that terrified me for years), I went out of the room, spinning the globe on my way, as I often did, mechanically, without giving it a thought. In the quiet house, my father probably wasn't there, the stairs creaked under my feet. In the middle of the kitchen lit by a neon strip, my mother looked lost and was crying quietly. She was rocking back and forth, biting her nails in front of three saucepans on the stove. These were days of funereal gloom and closed shutters. I stood in the doorway and she beckoned me over. Her ravaged face was streaked with make-up. I shuffled over the beige tiled floor in my socks. In the aroma of soup and leeks, the whistling valves, she put her arms around me and I cried, just to keep her company, I think, to show her I was there, by her side come what may. Eyes shut, tears running down my cheeks, I sniffled and quivered against her already thin body. After a long while, she stood up, wiped her eyes, nose and mouth with the material of her baggy dress, and apologised. I still don't know how to answer her, I have no idea why she wanted me to forgive her. I didn't know that a mother might one day ask her son for forgiveness.

WE SPENT THREE NIGHTS in Étretat. My father had reserved two rooms at the Hôtel des Corsaires, but we only used one. Perhaps it was Room 103, decorated differently but just as large, with a balcony if you wanted to stretch out in the fresh air.

On the first night, my brother, mother and I slept in the double bed. My father took one of the two armchairs. We hadn't drawn the curtains and the sun rose around eight o'clock. I remember the strong light and our eyes dazzled by the sea in the sunshine, the blinding whiteness of the cliffs. Mum got up first, opened the windows and leant out, wearing a pale nightdress. She hummed softly, shivering, as she gazed at the beach and chain-smoked cigarettes, the bright morning intoxicating.

She didn't leave the room during those two days in Étretat. She stayed on the balcony drinking tea, a book on her lap or perhaps a newspaper. She'd search the horizon, screwing up her eyes. Every now and then, she'd stand up, walk across the room, trailing her good hand behind her, lightly resting it on the wood of the furniture or our tousled hair as my brother and I played hangman or noughts-and-crosses.

Around midday, on the first day, my father popped out with my brother to buy something to make sandwiches. The next day I went with him. The streets set back from the sea were gloomy, their roughcast walls decorated with wood. We spent our afternoons on the beach, sometimes leaving it to explore the paths. In the west, towards Le Havre, lay the open moor, not yet eroded by the golf course. We'd walk beside meadows where rabbits hopped, we'd lean over the drop to make ourselves dizzy. In the east, cows chewed the cud in the fields where the chapel overlooked the village. I don't remember my father's face, how he reacted when my mother refused to come with us, preferring to stay in the hotel and take a siesta or simply read. All I remember is the turn of the key to lock her in, our silent walks, the wind, my fear we'd find her gone on our return. We'd come back in the evening light and she'd still be there, how could things have been different, how could she have disappeared, vanished into thin air, melted away? Lying in the middle of the bed, the curtains half-drawn, she beckoned us over and we snuggled up against her, she hugged us close singing in a low voice, and suddenly I was four again. The last rays of the sun sank into the water, softening the whiteness of the surrounding rocks, imparting a faint yellowish tinge. All this time, mum was very calm, quiet and probably dazed by the medication.

What I remember of the third night is the precise, yet re-created image of my mother's body falling through the darkness. We were sleeping on the balcony, Antoine and I, wrapped up warmly in our jackets, our four blankets, submerged in the belly of the sea. The sky was starless, dense and black, the night not so dark around the streetlamps. I recall never having felt so strongly that the sea was swelling, roaring, howling as everything around slept, swamping space and covering the world. Under the absent moon, my mother rose from the bed where my father was snoring. Softly she turned the key. She walked along the edge of the wide beach and we didn't see her. She went barefoot, transparent, wearing a long nightdress, the way she sometimes walked through the streets of the neighbourhood where we lived. (Like her, now, I often walk at night, wandering blindly through trees or by the sea, my hands brushing the bark, my heels scratched by brambles and heather, my skin chilled and wet, without knowing why, as waterlogged scents waft upwards. My father used to tell the neighbours that she was a sleepwalker and I believed him. Far from being reassured, I was terrified by this lie, because of the strange stories going round that anyone who woke her ran the risk of killing her.) The steep, dark path climbed sharply, my mother groped forward, stones jutted through the surface and soon her legs were covered with blood, scratches and dirt. A couple of paces from the sheer drop, she leant out over the black waters, the thick sea at the base of the dark rocks, charcoal grey at this hour. Spring was coming to a close, and my mother took another step: like a rubber puppet her body was washed up at low tide, skull and body smashed at the foot of the cliffs, covered with black sand, tiny pebbles, shells and mica.

I DON'T REMEMBER ANYTHING before all that. Either about my mother or myself. Nine years, from my birth to my first memory, have been swallowed without a trace. Everything before mum's death is blurred and fragmented. There are times when I wonder if everything I've forgotten is lodged somewhere. If all these accumulated events, words, feelings and gestures form a small part of me, if they provide me with a base of sorts, or if I've grown up over an abyss, the ground caving in beneath my feet. I have scores of photos, several reels of super-eight film, that show me as a child, that show her as I never knew her. Roaring with laughter, radiant. Armed with a bottle of water, chasing us round the garden, dancing in a sarong with orange flowers on the terrace of a holiday home. Light as air, she twirls in the sunshine, smokes at her bedroom window or behind the wheel of a car, hair tied back with a scarf and eyes hidden behind tinted glasses. As for me, I have a shock of pale blonde hair and most of the time I'm pouting. Dressed in flannel shorts and an orange T-shirt that leaves my midriff bare, I'm stroking a large russet dog, eating chips with my fingers, dazzled by the summer sun, looking into the camera presumably held by my father. Antoine and I roll in the grass, hurtle down slopes dotted with clover and daisies. At the foot of a tall cherry tree, we pretend to be musicians and our guitars are tennis racquets. On the living-room carpet we give military salutes, stiff as pokers, red plastic skimmers for helmets. I could go on with this list of photos studied thousands of times, photos of a childhood I don't remember having, traces of a buried life. I look at these photos and that fun-loving mother so full of life. I never knew her, she could be someone else's mother. And that sulky little boy, always hiding behind his mum's long dresses, or standing next to his beaming, dark-haired beanpole of a brother, could easily not be me. You could show me millions of photos of another sulky, fair-haired boy, who looked like me, and they would be just as *real*, just as vital, as the ones I have in my possession, and I could claim that they provided unique, unquestionable evidence of my childhood.

All that remains of the years before my mother's death is a misty stream of images, most of which smell of rain and damp earth, and take me back to the house where the four of us lived in that bleak, indeterminate town, without centre or outline, stuck between the Seine and the forest, a few miles from Paris. A house clinging to other identical houses, the same orange-tiled roofs, the same exposed stones, the same bare breeze-block garages with identical cars parked out front. I lived there until I was seventeen and, when I think back, what always comes to mind first are the damp November streets, then the smell of smoke, wet grass and pulped leaves, the sound of lawn-mowers in the spring, the tall grey towers nearby, looming over the artificial lake, the trunk road lined with signs and the strings of headlamps, and that entire vague, shared geography that means nothing to anyone who hasn't lived there. The RER station and the youth centre, the hospital and the Intermarché, the car park and the tatty lawn of the Youri-Gagarine estate, the PMU bar, the jobcentre, the cinema, the school playground and the chalk lines on the facades. The private housing estates and their immaculate lawns, smooth cement planted with scrawny trees and laurel hedges. And there, all that time, my brother on his bike with me on my skates hanging on to his saddle, football in the street on summer evenings, the tulips, the rusty garden furniture, the concrete paving, the walls bristling with broken glass, the rose bushes and the hose, our parents' bedroom with the shutters closed in the middle of the day, my father's taxi parked in front of the kitchen, the swing, the terrace and the barbecue, the garden with its neatly mown lawn before my mother's death and its tall grass after, the gloomy living room with its few pieces of furniture, its unadorned walls, the beige patterned wallpaper dotted with paintings from God knows where, yellowing ferns, sickly rubber plants, withered cut flowers, vases in imitation Chinese porcelain full of stale water. The scraggy red cedars and the lawn scorched in summer, dotted with patches of loose, brown earth in spring, pale, frozen and cracked in winter, the roar of the mopeds and the streetlamps leaning over the bitumen, glistening with drizzle and lined with Japanese flowering cherry trees, the kitchen with its pale wood furniture and my mother standing there, gazing into space, singing softly without noticing, staring at the window overlooking the street, or standing in front of the microwave as if completely engrossed in the circular motion of the plate in the light, or in the living room, pallid in the halogen glow and stooped over her ironing table, staring at the television set but looking somewhere beyond.

Dissolving into tears in the middle of the meal, when my father's family was there, or in front of programmes when she curled up between us on the velvet couch without paying any attention to the television. Her arms around us tight enough to smother us and her tears soaking into our hair.

Lying down in broad daylight, all day long, in the half-light of the closed shutters, a glove filled with hot water and Synthol on her forehead. Or in her car, parked on the verge when taking me to school, the stadium or the shopping centre, her eyes too misted with tears to see the road, her body shaking too much to avoid an accident.

Outside in the middle of the night—I'd watch her from my window when I couldn't sleep—crossing the garden with bare feet, sometimes in the rain, caressing tree trunks, burying her fingers in the earth, then walking into the street, moving further and further away and I never found out where she went.

She'd come back a few hours later and I still wasn't asleep, I'd be watching out for her from behind the curtains, her face would be spattered with mud and the material of her dress green with moss, her feet black, leaves in her hair; she'd probably walked as far as the river, sat on the banks beside that dark ribbon. Or she'd walked to the nearby forest; I picture her scratched by bushes, hugging the trunks of chestnut trees, eating earth perhaps, chewing leaves and ferns. Or perhaps she went to the wasteland a little further away, a fenced expanse of tall grass; we played football there with my brother and a few friends from the neighbourhood, it was summer and night was slow in coming. I don't know a thing about those nocturnal walks. I never dared ask her about them. All I know is that when she came back she didn't go to her own room but preferred to slip into my bed. I'd pretend to be asleep but I felt her damp, frozen skin against me.

Chatting in the living room, surrounded by neighbourhood acquaintances, mothers she'd met at the school gates and whom she occasionally, rarely, invited over for tea and cake, their children in tow, with whom we played in the garden. I don't know what they could have found to talk about, those anonymous women and my reserved, too-fragile mother with her bitten nails, little tags of nibbled skin around mother-of-pearl dotted with white patches.

If I want to describe my childhood and the little I remember about it, my mother and the little I know about her, I must talk about the emptiness after my father set off, the acrid smell of the mornings and the silence that pervaded the house on Wednesdays and during the holidays, or when I was ill (which was quite often, I think), and I stayed on my own with her. A terrible sadness invaded the space, drying out the texture of the air, altering the smells. It felt as if everything were suddenly suspended, caught in a hiatus, an asthmatic pause, a hesitation. A sadness wreathed in fog, like an endless November, froze us from inside and a lump rose in my throat for no apparent reason. On those mornings, my mother would wander through the house, useless and ashen, walking from one room to another without doing anything, heating water in a saucepan on the stove then forgetting it, sweeping or mopping the floor although everything was spotless, straightening anything that was barely out of place. She'd turn on the radio, then the television, which showed a constant stream of poorly dubbed television series filled with candles, leather sofas, flower arrangements and fireplaces. Preoccupied, she'd barely glance at them, get up from the armchair, leaving the television on just for the noise. Sometimes, she'd make a phone call and, from my room, I could hear her choked voice. I don't know who she could have been talking to. She didn't have any female friends that I knew of, or any family. I'd stay in bed and wait for the time to pass. Or, sitting cross-legged on the living room carpet, I'd flick through well-thumbed comics, *Gaston Lagaffe* and *Boule et Bill*, *Les Tuniques bleues*, *Achille Talon*, *Lucky Luke*. The house smelt of detergent, the light filtering in was cold and harsh, and the silence had a threatening ring.

I must also describe the evenings, homework in the kitchen, the spinning steam valves and the smell of soup everywhere. The television game *Numbers and Letters* turned down low, *Animals of the World* on Sunday evenings, the oven shedding light on a courgette gratin. Maths and grammar. The recitation pieces, the blotting paper. The exercise-book covers. And my mother behind her ironing table, iron in hand in the living room. From time to time I look at her; I can see her from where I am. Her eyes cloud over and, suddenly, she raises the iron in a horizontal position, stands stock-still for seconds that last hours and it occurs to me that she's wavering between gliding the iron across the fabric or pressing it to her face, burning her skin, cheekbones, eyes and forehead. At night, regularly, for too many years to count, I was terrified by the image of her half-melted, crimson face.

Lastly, I must describe her awkward, extravagant gestures of affection which always came at the wrong time (as did the slaps, the shouting, the lectures, as if she'd suddenly snapped back to reality, how we wore her out and what on earth had she done to deserve children like this?—the bouts of depression and, again, her laughter, her infrequent cuddles, then the looks she gave us, as if tinged with guilt for being affectionate). And the handful of images I have of her that are serene rather than happy, all of them ironically linked to the sea. They are fleeting images, light and gentle as a hand caressing a face. They are bound up with how thin she was towards the end, something I didn't realise then, but is very noticeable in the photos. They are bound up with her silence in the last few months, when she hardly ever emerged from her room. My mother had stopped eating, had stopped taking meals with us because, she said, she had been nibbling while cooking, and also because she wasn't "very hungry this evening". I have no idea how my father reacted to all this. Did he force her to eat? Did he drag her to the doctor? Did he order her to take care of herself, pull herself together, leave her room and the warm gloves filled with Synthol, get out and meet people, find some *activities*, go to the cinema or join one of the pottery, drawing, patchwork or silk-painting workshops at the local community centre advertised on posters pinned to wooden telegraph poles with birds perched on their taut wires and piles of tattered paper turned to papier-mâché by the rain around their base?

My mother was fading away and that last summer my father rented an ochre roughcast house on the hilltops with a view over orange rocks plunging into the sea, arbutus and cork oaks. To the east, a crescent of beach stretched away in the sharp, intense light. Further off, there were villas, a line of hotels, fluorescent signs, three-star campsites, beaches and crimson porphyry inlets, obese palm trees in rows, bars with unlit neon signs. The terrace overlooked the bay. A marine pine towered above the garden carpeted with pine needles. I pressed my forehead against the hot bark, peeled off strips, and sap oozed onto my fingers. The living room had a strong smell of dust and old wood, salt and dry stone, which sometimes comes back to me. It always gives me a pang and catches me by surprise, marks me as its own and overwhelms me.

The day would dawn already warm and shrouded in a greyish-pink halo. Mum would open the shutters and spend the morning on the terrace drinking China tea, a book or a copy of *Elle* in her hand. The water sparkled as far as the eye could see. She lit menthol cigarettes, tipping back in her chair as she watched the birds circling high above, on the lookout for croissant crumbs, bits of bread or brioche on the ground. Sometimes she got up from her chair and went for a short stroll in the garden, stroking the leaves with a trailing hand, the tall grass, the trunk, bark and stone. Around midday, my father would take out the portable barbecue and begin grilling sardines or meat. After coffee, we would go down to the beach. There was a path leading down to the sand, the little snack bar and the beached pedalos. It was lined on either side with laurel hedges. Through them, you could see swimming pools, garden furniture on terraces, abandoned children's toys, towels drying. The scents of liquorice and dried herbs floated on the air. Antoine and I would dash along the path, followed by our parents; we'd wait for them breathlessly, our temples burning, impatient to dive into the water. Mum never bathed, she would just walk up and down the sand, her dress lifted halfway up her thighs, her bare feet in the still water. Some days, Antoine and I continued as far as the inlets. The sheer rocks plunged straight down into the limpid water. Trees clung on somehow, grass, brambles and bushes grew on the bare rock. We went barefoot along the paths. We ran with red knees and scorched fingers among the white-hot rocks, our hair plastered with sweat, our towels rolled around our necks. The sun burned our eyelids. We hung our clothes from the branches of a tree, dived head first into the turquoise water and swam to the islands. The others were already there, chewing slivers of wood, smoking, gazing at the blue sky, talking about everything and nothing, their expressions very serious, absently running their hands over their already brown torsos.

We'd return home in the evening light, mum would be lying down and would beckon us over. We snuggled up to her, one on either side; she stroked our hair singing, as she did a year later in the locked room, with the view of the cliffs at Étretat. From there, we watched the sun dying over the bluish-grey water, setting fire to the red overhanging rocks. With the curtains this created an orange light. Mum dozed, soft and relaxed, and I can still hear her voice singing over the old Billie Holiday records she played one after the other, all day long.

I'VE LEFT MY MOST UNCLOUDED MEMORIES cradled in a summer house. A month went by in the warmth of the air, the light was a caress and when we left the terrace, the view of the bay, mum hid herself away and cried. A few weeks later, she burned her left hand and it was on purpose. I was there, not far from her in the living room when she did it. I was drawing on the coffee table, squatting on the light brown carpet. She was ironing in the bleak morning light with the television on for no one. For minutes on end, she stared at the window and the garden beyond, the lawn edged by sickly red cedars. I looked up and she was standing motionless, her right hand in the air and the iron held in a horizontal position, as it was so often in the evening, in my darkest dreams. Her left hand was placed flat on the board in its moss-green cover with orange flowers. Very slowly, she brought the iron closer to her hand and it was if I'd been turned to stone. I wanted to scream but no sound came out. She pressed down and her mouth twisted into a grimace. Her skin began to burn, melt, filling the room with the stench of burnt meat. She remained silent, stoical, except for the agonised expression on her face. Time stretched endlessly, each second seeming as substantial as a day. A slow-motion film was unfolding in front of my eyes and my mother was a shadow on the screen. Antoine came in and I looked at him in tears—that was all I could do. He screamed and rushed over to her. She fell into his arms, as if she were dead. He kissed her eyes and her forehead, cradled her tightly against him, rocking her the way you soothe an upset child. I watched him murmuring panic-stricken phrases, prayers. I couldn't move a muscle.

The ambulance arrived and my mother was taken to the Salpêtrière burns unit, before being transferred to a psychiatric clinic, somewhere in the Essonne region. I didn't see her for six months. Not until the day we went to collect her, my father, Antoine and I. The day we drove through the night in the silent car, towards Étretat and its cliff-lined stretches, as if we were a strange cortège accompanying her to her own death.

I KNOW NOTHING OR VERY LITTLE about my mother before I was born. Or about her early years or how she met my father. I don't have any details about the moves that took her from the Aveyron region, where she lived for part of her childhood, to the Porte d'Orléans in Paris, where she and her parents rented a tiny flat on the sixth floor of a red-brick block. We drove past it from time to time, on the rare occasions we went into Paris to see a film starring Belmondo or Pierre Richard or to admire the Christmas lights. She'd point out two windows and always come out with the same story about doing her homework on a makeshift desk made by placing a plank of wood on top of the washbasin. She'd add that four of them lived like this in a single room after what she mysteriously called her father's "ruin". I don't know what type of business her father was in or how he earned a living after things turned out badly. Nor do I know how old she was when she left school and the family flat, if she passed her baccalaureate or not, or even if she sat it. I was too young to be interested in things like that. I didn't begin to ask such questions until much later, when there was no longer any way of finding out the answers. Since then, I've given up trying to fill in the gaps. When it comes down to it, what I know about my mother is lodged somewhere else, in my stomach and my blood, under each square centimetre of my skin.

After she died, she was always with me, living by my side, saturating each moment with her presence, each particle of air with her memory and the mystery of my honeycombed memory. She visited me for years, day and night, and she still sometimes does today. In the early years, her almost daily apparitions transcended dreams and nightmares, recollections or memory, and entered the realm of hallucination. Of course, I dreamt about her and she was alive, she talked to me, smiled at me, ran her fingers through my hair, took my hand and led me through the forest, trees dripping from a recent shower, she stood on tiptoe and caught tiny droplets of water on the tip of her tongue. Or she was walking in the sea, her dress lifted just above her knees, as I had seen her do many times that last summer. Soon the material was soaking and she licked the salt from it then, letting it fall, she slowly walked deeper and deeper into the water until she completely disappeared, shoulders face and hair gradually submerged. Or lying on a sandy beach in Brittany, beside the rising water, again motionless and smiling with the smile of a saint in ecstasy, eyes fixed on the sky thick with birds, letting herself be submerged, the salt water covered her slowly, flooding her eyes, her lungs. Her hands burrowed into the ground, the grains of sand worked their way under her skin, into the cracks, and scored her eyes like diamonds on glass, body and face sanded, eroded by salt, filed down to the bone.

But it wasn't enough for my mother to live and die by night beneath my eyelids, drowned in water or buried by sand. She was continually appearing to me, a small, pale, diaphanous phantom, in a barely discernible but indisputable flash, when I went into the kitchen, the living room or her bedroom. I *really* thought I saw her at those times. I'd blink and she'd disappear, leaving nothing behind but a heart-rending memory, the cruel disappointment after a mirage. Also sometimes, outside, I'd distinctly hear her voice calling me, speaking in my ear or I'd hear her crying. I think now that I was living in a different world. I'd taken up residence there, untroubled by any particular grief or misery, with virtually no cries of distress or attacks of violent sobbing, virtually no rolling around on the floor, banging my head against the kitchen cupboards, punching the cement walls hundreds of times. The torpor induced by the sedatives prescribed by our family doctor had me living in muffled lands, in an unfocused part of my brain, completely divorced from real life, as if I were on another floor, in another room, in a continuous past where my mother wasn't dead.

IN THE WARM ROOM, the air is filled with the scent of my daughter, the smell of her mother. I lie down beside them. Chloé groans and I breathe in her hair, her smell of soap, blackcurrant and milk. I kiss her neck, her tiny fingers, her shoulder. She opens her eyes for a second, murmurs "Papa" and immediately goes back to sleep.

It's now two years since she was born, since she has been by my side, keeping me safe. Two years and I often feel that nothing existed before, nothing happened, as if once again my memory is double-locking itself and dragging the past thirty years into a hidden place in my brain. A place that no longer has any importance.

Her face is pale in the light suffusing the room. Pallid streetlamps line the concrete of the beachside promenade littered with restaurants, bars and children's play areas. I stand up again and there are times when I say to myself that the past is a fiction, that you can wipe the slate clean, that you can build on top of ruins and live without foundations. There are also times when I believe the opposite.

The precise feel of Claire's hands squeezing mine is what I remember of Chloé's birth. Her fingers were twisting my fingers, working their way in between them, and I could sense her fear. The fear of Chloé being born, then the fear of someone taking her away in the same impulse. That is something Claire and I have always shared, I think, from the very beginning. The clear, terrified image of everything slipping away. Of something that, being born, begins dying or threatens to vanish. Claire was resting and Chloé was an incredibly fragile, violet thing, her eyes opened and closed sporadically, and for three days she coughed up mucus, an abundance of yellow, viscous gunk. Tubes burrowed into the tiny veins on her flushed arms; others ran under her nose, providing oxygen. I remember thinking, at the sight of the panicked hospital staff in those first minutes of her life, when I realised she was barely breathing, that she was in pain and that they were violently massaging her torso and stomach, pressing her crumpled, still soiled skin with impatient hands, I remember thinking: 'No, you can't, you can't do that to her,' and that thought was a frantic prayer. A prayer for Claire and not for me or Chloé. Even now I wonder what that appeal meant and whom it was really for.

Chloé grunts a little, moves her head from left to right and sinks back into sleep. I think that almost losing her at birth has significantly shaped my attachment to her, my inability to stand by and watch her suffer or even be sad or just dissatisfied. My own life is probably also mixed up with all that. Probably. I softly close the window. There is a couple kissing under the balcony. The man looks up for a second, notices me and gives an amused nod. I slip back under the blankets and the cold air bites into my face. All along the beach, the last few restaurants are closing, the signs are switching off. All that's left is the sea, the beating of the waves, the dark sky.

I WAS ELEVEN BUT WHEN I THINK BACK to the funeral, or the little I remember of it, I tell myself that I must have been six or seven. I recall such a lack of distress, grief, such a lack of comprehension. It was as if I were watching an odd enactment, an absurd performance in which the actors were my father, assorted uncles and aunts whom I've never seen since, and my brother, rigid as a ramrod, eyes bulging and mute. I never believed that the long coffin made of varnished wood contained my mother's mangled body. I still don't believe it. When I think about that rectangle six feet under, I distinctly hear the dull, dry sound of the spadefuls of earth under which she disappeared, but I'm still convinced that either there's nothing inside or it contains a wax dummy or, even, mysteriously, the years that were stolen from me. I often tell myself that the first years of my life are not completely lost, just buried under pounds of brown earth, somewhere at the bottom of a hole, enclosed by four wooden planks, inaccessible and at the same time easy to exhume. So trying to force open my closed memory seems like an unacceptable act of desecration.

My mother was buried on a morning of harsh light and abrasive sunshine. A ceremony was held in an ugly cube-shaped church at the corner of two streets, between a chemist and an estate agent, near a hoarding for Saint-Maclou floorings. I remember my red-faced, sweating uncles in their tight black suits, polished shoes, my aunts with their smeared makeup. Even then, I sensed they would always do their utmost to avoid us, to make sure they didn't know how we were coping, how we would live, the three of us, with a mother who'd committed suicide, a wife who'd fallen apart. As if our unhappiness could contaminate them, spread to them, bring death, madness, depression. It was also then that I realised, from their crass mask-like features as they drove along the trunk road, that they'd always hated her and her strange behaviour, her bird-like airs.

Even so, clustered around the entrance to the church—opposite the cinema showing *Who's That Girl?*—I suppose we must have looked like a family in mourning, seen from the passing cars. The undertaker's assistants had obsequious manners, sad, suitable smiles; Antoine was unsteady on his legs, the others wore fitting expressions, and my father gritted his teeth. I don't recall what suddenly made him hit his brother as they stood there on the square in front of the church, causing blood to spurt from his nose. All I remember is my uncle yelling, my aunts and an older cousin grabbing him by the waist, his flushed, furious face a couple of inches from the black hearse with tinted windows. My uncle leaving, walking back to his Renault 18, followed by his indignant little family. We went into the church and, sitting in silence on the uncomfortable pews, blowing on our freezing hands, we waited for the coffin to be brought in to the accompaniment of a shrill organ.

Everything slid off me like water down a pane of glass. I wasn't there, I didn't know what people were talking about, I wondered where my mother was, what was inside that long box made of varnished wood, when she would come back, when this would all be over, this bad dream, this cruel joke. Sitting in the front row, I stared at the blue and orange abstract patterns of the stained-glass windows, and Antoine held my hand. He was listening attentively to what was being said by the priest, a young friendly-looking man, whose lips were shaping words that didn't reach my ears. I couldn't take my eyes off my brother and his eyes were shining, tears welled up without falling, forming a translucent, gelatinous film, a lens of salt water. Then suddenly he toppled over, crumpling in a heap, limp as a rag. Noiselessly, the inside of his body dissolved, leaving only a thin, frameless husk. Dragged over by his weight, I fell with him and the priest broke off what he was saying. A wave of murmurs engulfed me. People were looking at us, me on the ground completely bemused, and my brother, eyes closed, in a dead faint. My father leant over us and I can still see his expression, the anger in his face, as if we had simply been up to some mischief. He shook my brother, slapped him twice, but Antoine remained motionless, laid out in the middle of the rows, looking delicate and graceful, his head lolling against the cold floor. Help arrived quickly, the priest held my hand and assured me there was nothing to worry about, that everything would be fine. Just before my father left, he asked the priest to continue with the ceremony. He whispered a few words to one of his sisters, in whose care he left me, and I watched him disappear, heading out into the street and daylight, the lifeless body of my brother in his arms. I was left alone with a family full of strangers, my hand clamped in the damp, fleshy hand of an obese aunt.

In her car, on the way to the cemetery, no one made the slightest sound and this silence became one in my mind with the silence that numbed our mornings when I was a kid and my mother wandered near to tears through the house. These silences combine to produce a cold, acrid noise that makes my throat and eyes sting when I hear it, the noise of an engine or still life, a deserted house, time standing still, which, when I'm in a car or any other place, makes me turn on the music to drown it out and which, at night, makes me go out to get high on the whistling of the wind, the din of the sea, the commerce of the birds or the rustling of the leaves.

Antoine and my father didn't come back. The funeral carried on without them. Only I watched the box disappear into that gruesome hole, only I studied the indifference of my uncles, aunts, cousins, only I saw the rose land on the wood, the first spadefuls of earth gradually cover it, only I saw myself throw up against a tree, without hiccups without tears and without cries, the way you empty yourself endlessly, the way life leaves you, deserts you, and hurls you once and for all into a winter without end.

AFTER ALL THAT, THEY DROPPED ME HOME. The house was deserted and plunged into darkness, at least that's how I picture it, although it was broad daylight and a sharp sun was sandpapering the sky. How could my aunt have left me alone? I was eleven and they had just buried my mother. I remember feeling suddenly tiny and as if I'd broken into somebody else's house. I tiptoed around, as though it were pitch black, touched the walls, held on to the furniture. I stayed in the living room for a long time, lying in the middle of the carpet with my eyes closed. What was I thinking about then? Probably my mother, my brother. What was left of him? Where had they taken him? Where were they hiding them? I spent several hours like this, unmoving in the unbroken silence, and I think, in my heart of hearts, that the reason I wasn't crying was because tears were flooding me on the inside, submerging my organs my heart my blood my viscera my lungs, turning me to liquid and rain.

A sour, greyish evening set in. I went to throw up many times as dusk lingered on. The stairs emitted sinister creaks, like dead wood, like trees brought down in a storm. The door gave a long groan, opening on to a spotless, depressing bedroom. I never set foot in there, we were forbidden by my father. During the day, mum closed the shutters and lay down in the partial half-light. Sometimes she spoke our names softly. We'd hear her voice from our quiet rooms. She would beckon us in, ask us how our day had been, if everything was all right at school. Outside, the daylight throbbed, you could see it through the chinks, the birch swayed, impaled by sunshine, branches chiselled by light. Going into that room without permission, when my parents weren't there, was unreal. I felt as if I were entering a museum, a room that was off-limits, a burial site. Everything in it seemed dead and my mother was dead and perhaps my brother was too, I couldn't help thinking that he might also have died, that life had drained out of him, leaving only the limp rag of his skin. That was when I saw my first apparition. I sensed a presence behind me, a hand on my shoulder. I turned round and saw my mother's face, for a fraction of a second, I swear, I saw her face and she was smiling. She disappeared almost immediately. I began to cry. That was when it started, only then. I cried for a long time. Until my eyes were burning, until I felt dizzy and exhausted. Lying flat on my stomach, my teeth biting into the sheets and pillow. My mouth left deep, wet circles, neat rows of teeth marks.

Later in the evening, I began emptying my mother's cupboards and drawers. I took out dresses, skirts and blouses. Tears ran down my wet cheeks and I swallowed pints of mucus. The clothes piled up, a ridiculous, pathetic pyramid without a tomb. Armed with large sewing scissors, I cut everything into pieces. I did it calmly, assiduously, breathing deeply to catch my breath. Tangled fragments, garlands of multicoloured material piled up in the suitcases, which I threw one by one crashing downstairs in a commotion of wood and plastic. I emptied them over the living room carpet. It was dark and a single orange lamp lit the room, its dreary wallpaper, its dark wood furniture covered in doilies, fruit bowls and knick-knacks. I put on the record that mum loved so much, 'California Dreamin'. It kept playing on and on and soon there was a pile three-foot-high. With the newspaper that my father kept in stacks in the shed, I lit a fire in the grate. Using heavy black cast-iron tongs, I burned the scraps of material one by one. Some gave off a black smoke, a chemical smell that prickled my eyes and stuck in my throat. I don't know what significance these actions had for me, or even if they meant anything at all.

Everything had been reduced to ashes when the phone rang. I picked up the receiver and it was my father, he would be home soon. My brother was in a coma, at the Villeneuve-Saint-Georges Hospital. His condition was stable and inexplicable.

M Y FATHER CAME BACK, it was midnight and I was pretending to be asleep on the living-room sofa. The fire had gone out but there was a lingering smell of burnt wood and fabric. The suitcases were put away in the cupboards, the scissors in the sewing box, and on several occasions as I was dozing, I'd thought I felt mum's breath on my forehead or heard her footsteps on the stairs. When I opened my eyes there was nothing there. I soon became convinced that ghosts, or at any rate my mother's ghost, have a premonition when the people they are visiting suddenly become aware of their presence and they disappear in a flash. I spent many years playing with her, trying to catch her out, opening my eyes suddenly, blinking very fast. On several occasions, I managed to catch a glimpse of her.

My father never made any reference to my mother's clothes. That evening, after closing the living-room shutters, he went upstairs to Antoine's room. I imagine that he filled a bag with a change of clothes. I fell asleep with a feeling of complete emptiness.

When I woke, my father ordered me to hurry up and get dressed, we were leaving for the hospital. My brother was sleeping perfectly still on his bed of pale blue sheets. There was a pane of glass separating us from him and the machines measuring all kinds of things with the aid of electrodes stuck to his chest. Thin, translucent tubes slid under his skin. With his bare torso, his hair plastered to his forehead, Antoine looked just like a little boy. He suddenly seemed so frail, so delicate. My father stared intently at him, watching for a sign, a movement. I think he suspected him of faking it. I caught myself searching his face and body for tiny changes, for minute tremors that would expose him and give his secret away. I was also sure of it: my brother was 'pretending' to sleep. Not to be a pain in the neck, which is what my father thought. But to make sure he was left in peace. Left alone to grieve. So that he could keep his eyes shut and preserve images of my mother intact on his retina. So that he would forget nothing. Lose nothing. Keep everything bottled up inside so that nothing could escape.

For the duration of his coma, six weeks in total, and for a long time after he was moved to a room where I could sit next to him and listen to his breathing, whisper in his ear, kiss his face and rest his hand on mine, I don't think I budged in my conviction: he was play-acting, he was 'playing dead'. We came to visit him and my father never stayed long. He went outside to smoke a cigarette, make a phone call, or went off to work and collected me on his return. I spent hours at my brother's bedside, sometimes entire days: Wednesdays, Saturdays, Sundays. The room was blue and various nurses came in to change the tubes, the drips, the nappies they put him in. Sometimes I had to leave the room and there were patients in slippers wandering about in the corridors. Their families smoked and paced up and down near the windows. I'd go to the machine to buy some chocolate. During this time, they washed my brother and he let them, heavy and limp, floppy and difficult to manoeuvre. From a distance, they would signal that I could go back into the room. I'd sit down in the large armchair that I'd dragged over to the bed. I studied his face, I spent long hours just watching him. Or I whispered to him. Most of the time, I told him about my days at school. No one ever talked to me and the teachers didn't like me. Sometimes I also tested him. I told him dirty jokes, came out with all kinds of swear words or horrifying remarks, tickled his feet, or his face with a feather. I waited for him to smile, purse his lips, wrinkle his forehead or twitch his nostrils, anything that would give him away. Once I even murmured in his ear: "Mum's back." But the only signs of life my brother gave for six weeks were his perfectly regular breathing and the movement of his eyeballs under the darkness of his eyelids, something I'd gradually learnt to spot. It showed when he was dreaming and when, in all probability, my mother was with him, smiling at him or kissing his hair.

Those six weeks went by in a flash, a nauseating, unsettled flash, heavy with the breath of my brother's deep sleep, suffused with hospital light, the bland light of sky-blue walls and neon strips, six weeks filled with the smell of ether and cold soup, surgical spirit and industrial detergent, with the careworn faces of surly nurses, six weeks perched in that long building overlooking blocks of flats towering above the river, the thick, bronze Seine, the headlamps of lanes of cars, queuing bumper to bumper on the outskirts of the city. Six weeks and the sun setting on the hills in the distance, lined with buildings and ridges that looked like rectangles of Lego. The sky wore different hues, tawny or lemony, dark purple or phosphorescent, cracked violently, streaked by the vapour trails of planes taking off from Orly airport nearby. My brother slept without moving, the sheet pulled over his bare torso, deep in a causeless, inexplicable coma that was impervious to all the diagnoses, prognoses, analyses given by doctors impressive in their white coats, their jargon, their silvery temples, their well-groomed skin, their aura of success.

My brother woke one evening and, to my great surprise, there wasn't anything stranger or more extraordinary about it than two eyes opening and taking in their surroundings, the walls and the window, the swaying trees, the sky in the distance, crackled red and creamy blue that evening, the furniture, then me, sitting in the large armchair under the wall-mounted television. He smiled weakly at me, closed his eyes for a minute. When he opened them again, I was right by his side.

"You were pretending, weren't you? You weren't actually in a coma, were you?"

He turned to me, still half-asleep. He looked at me for a long time, his eyes studying my face, without reproach, without irony, without sadness. All they contained was weariness and anxiety. In a groggy voice, he asked where mum was. From the expression on his face, I realised that after six weeks out of it, he was hoping with all his heart that he'd just had a bad dream. He was hoping that the blankness and the black hole into which he'd fallen had obliterated everything, had washed everything away, that the world was new and had started over, and that our mother was still alive and hadn't thrown herself from the cliff top. Very slowly, I said those irrefutable words: "Mum's dead". And tears ran down my brother's face.

I didn't tell the nurses. I was alone with my brother in that room with the glossy walls, we were two motherless children in the midst of a vast hospital, a desert of hills, blocks of flats, and planes passing each other in the sky, housing estates, vast car parks and railway networks. I took off my shoes and lay next to him in the narrow bed. He wanted to put his arms round me but he was too weak, his limbs were limp, his body emaciated, his sunken stomach showed his protruding ribs.

II

ALL THE LIGHTS OFF

I LIGHT ANOTHER FOUR CANDLES. I arrange them on the low plastic table. The flames quiver, threatening to go out at any moment. It's a cheap ritual, a ridiculous ceremony, my petty settlements with the dead, with my mother who fell there, directly in my line of vision. The beach is deserted and the lights illuminating the cliffs have just gone out. They are now just barely discernible masses, dark shapes against the darkness of the night, superimposed textures, cotton on silk.

The plate-glass window is half-opened and Claire's face appears. She is cold and is lightly rubbing her arms, which she keeps crossed over her chest. Her face glows in the shadows, and her nightdress flutters around her light, solid body. She leans over and kisses me.

"Can't you sleep?"

"They've just turned out the cliffs."

She pokes her tongue between my teeth and I run my fingers over her backside, my hands are cold and she shivers. I offer her a mouthful of whisky; she glances at the half-empty bottle. She doesn't say anything. She has been by my side for so long now, years and years and never, never has she made the slightest remark about the large quantities of alcohol I knock back and which I know keep me on my feet, plug the gaps and raise me up again, protect me and anaesthetise me. Nor has she ever shown any surprise at my nocturnal walks. Not even when I undress in the early hours and press my icy body against her warm skin. She brings her mouth close to my lips, breathes in my smell of tobacco, fern, salt and vodka, pulls me into her embrace and we reel in the breaking dawn.

"I'm going back to bed."

Her hand lingers on my face and she disappears into the room, rejoins Chloé who drowsily demands some milk. Claire rocks her and her singing is drowned out by the waves and the tumbled shingle.

Two years before Chloé was born, we left Paris, our crooked flat with its yellowing walls, its uneven floor covered with orange hexagonal tiles. Our windows with a view of the courtyard and, opposite, the mute dormers that showed silhouettes, bodies and faces that had become familiar. I'd spent entire nights and wasted days gazing at them, discovering their little habits, their repetitive actions. The elderly woman on the fourth floor went to bed around eight o'clock in the evening. Wearing a pink nightgown, her hair covered with a kind of bonnet, she would read late into the night, her poodle at her feet, and I'd doze off before her. Claire snored and I thought it was delightful, everything about her moved me, her radiant face, her crystalline laugh, the way she watched over me and forgave me, without complaining or asking for anything in return. For months after Léa's death, I had turned my back on any form of activity, I became like a parasite, a burdensome larva, my blood swam with alcohol, various psychotropic drugs floated in it, there were times when I didn't say a word all day, but Claire didn't pass comment. She came in late from work and we ate by candlelight. We made love on the couch, music on loud and her mouth felt cool. She'd collapse with exhaustion and I'd turn down the volume of the record that was playing, she'd sleep and I'd listen to sad, slow songs one after the other. Most of the time, my head was completely empty, I was incapable of holding a thought, I pressed my forehead against the cold window, I watched my neighbours, the student on the fifth floor glued to his computer and haloed with unreal light, the little old man on the third floor who ironed charcoal grey trousers in his boxer shorts, showing off scrawny legs covered with large purple veins. The young woman on the second floor, smoking in her kitchen, the newspaper open on the table, her eyes gazing into space, and earlier in the evening I'd seen her with a child in pyjamas, hair damp and brushed back after bath time, eating steaming hot soup and smiling at each other from time to time.

I'd doze off as the early morning noise was slowly getting louder outside. In a semi-coma, strangely frozen stiff, I'd hear Claire get out of bed, turn on the shower and make coffee. Then the door slammed shut on the silence and I sank into a deep, dreamless sleep.

This is what our life was like at first. I don't know where Claire found the strength to keep my head above water, to gaze at me lovingly with such indulgence, fairness and affection, where she hid her reserves of patience, intelligence and cheerfulness. We left Paris and it was like escaping from a dead city. All the people I met there were like my neighbours, shadows reduced to exhaustion, the monotonous daily grind. The city was suffocating me and every one of its streets seemed branded with memory and loss. Claire kept saying that we had to leave, we "had to escape". She wanted to smell the sea, smell it every day, every minute, whenever she wanted. She was also shouldering her burden of ghosts. She was deeply affected by Léa's death, even if she never talked about it. Léa's death had wounded her more deeply than I had thought, and even now I don't understand the true nature of the bond between them. We never know anything about the bonds that develop between people; often they don't know what they are themselves, and they only find out when they lose each other.

CLIFFS

One day in May, we moved into a tiny farmstead, a stone's throw from the deserted, windswept moors, where birds and carrier currents drifted. Claire had tears in her eyes, and something finally unclenched inside me, seemed to gain the will to survive. We looked at each other like two astonished children, and another life began.

A WEEK AFTER HE WOKE UP, Antoine came home. He didn't say a word for two months. Until the summer holidays. He still went to school during that time though. He attended lessons and, although he didn't apply himself any more diligently than before, no one hassled him. His classmates had been forewarned and this created an aura of mystery and respect around him that only grew over the years. His motherless status was heightened by the enigma of his silence and our mother's shocking suicide, our father's terrifying reputation and a wide range of crimes: expulsions, detentions, brawls, unexplained absences, insults to teachers, carrying and using a Stanley knife, cigarettes, alcohol and joints in the school grounds, broken windows in the school library, beating up a supervisor, ransacking the office in the childcare centre, and so on. In conjunction with this there were a handful of records in swimming and athletics and a few unexpected flashes of brilliance in History and French. Some of the teachers looked at him askance, as if to stress that, like my father, they weren't fooled by his 'little game' but, on the whole, everyone was very understanding and patient. Antoine was excused from speaking in class and no one ever refused him permission to go to the infirmary. From the window of my baking-hot classroom, I'd see him sauntering across the playground, lighting a cigarette and puffing long trails of smoke skywards. Classmates sitting near me also spotted him and nervous laughter rippled through the room. Mme Dausse shook her head and, although she didn't say anything, it was obvious she suspected I was taking advantage of the situation, making the most of it. I was eleven and my mother was dead. With hindsight, I tell myself that, really, I never did anything that measured up to my grief during that time. My brother took care of that side of things. The corridors were deserted and the inner windows revealed a procession of faces, some diligent, others dreamy, backs bent over double-width squared sheets of paper, eyes fixed on green boards covered with chalk. I left the midnight-blue prefabs and joined my brother near the cycle sheds. Buckled wheels were chained to rusty poles. Antoine would wait for me there and crush his fag end with the tip of his shoe. Before leaving school, we'd sometimes make a detour. The teachers' cars gleamed at the rear of the buildings, close to the gym and the unsupervised gate, which could easily be jumped, and then we were free. Antoine didn't choose his victims, he worked at random. I kept watch while he took a Stanley knife from his pocket and plunged it neatly into the tyres of a blue Renault 20 or a black Golf. He sometimes also ran his keys down the new paintwork with a screech, or broke a window with a stone.

We never went straight home. The town seemed uninhabited, a dormitory in broad daylight. Buses drove past with no passengers, infrequent shops languished with boredom in the deserted afternoon. We walked past empty houses, neglected tennis courts, gardens guarded by bad-tempered dogs. My brother stubbornly kept quiet and we sometimes signed to each other. I was incapable of opening my mouth when I was with him, as if I'd been contaminated. The cemetery was bare in the sunlight. Little old men gazed at slabs thick with dust, mauve flowers withering in pots. Our mother's unadorned tomb was there. We stared at it, hands crossed, and Antoine chewed on inaudible words.

We put off going home as long as possible. Our father didn't get home until dark. Antoine heated water and cooked vegetables. We played mum's records before he arrived. After that there was unbroken silence and my father, sitting at the head of the table, stolidly chewing his meat, wouldn't talk to us, he'd just shake his aggrieved head when he locked eyes with Antoine and bark: "Couldn't you find anything better to make yourself interesting? Believe you me, a clip round the ear will soon help you find your tongue."

Once the meal was over I cleared the table and my father sat down in front of the television. He wouldn't tolerate any noise and always ended up falling asleep. Once the crockery was dried and put away, I joined Antoine in his room. Sitting at his desk, he had his back to me and I put my hand on his shoulder. He swivelled his seat round and smiled at me, eyes still misted with tears. Side by side on his bed, we'd read comics until late, we'd listen to the radio softly, blindly following dark football matches between Lens and Laval.

Then summer arrived and my brother started talking again as though nothing had happened. It was so sudden and so natural that I don't remember the exact circumstances of this miracle. I think he asked me to pass the salt when we were eating and, when I handed it to him, he let slip an innocuous "thanks", which didn't even provoke a reaction from my father.

THIS MARKED THE START of a cold, intimidating time. For four years, we lived in an obsessive silence that nothing was allowed to disrupt. For four years, we haunted that house like ghosts, without speaking during the meals we ate in front of the television. For four years, we escaped our exasperated father's wrath by taking refuge in our bedrooms, where we'd get together even after 'curfew', while he snored in the living room. He always fell asleep in front of the film or variety shows, Patrick Sébastien Jean-Pierre Foucault Michel Drucker. We'd whisper, and I don't remember now what murmured secrets we shared. Sometimes our father caught us red-handed and yelled at me to go back to my room, threatening to give me a good hiding or beat me to a pulp there and then. I don't know how we could have been disturbing him. I think he wished we were dead. Dead and stuffed.

We were never supposed to make a noise or raise our voices, we were never supposed to laugh or whisper or tickle each other or chase each other round the house, we were never supposed to listen to music or talk to him about anything. We were never supposed to take longer than three seconds to obey one of his orders, we were never supposed to answer back, express an opinion contrary to his, or have an opinion at all. We weren't supposed to play in the garden, trample his lawn, kick the ball onto his flowers. We weren't supposed to touch his hi-fi, especially not break a plate or glass, and woe betide us if he heard our footsteps upstairs when he was sitting in the living room. We weren't supposed to bring home any friends, girls or boys, we weren't supposed to mix with black, mixed-race or Arab children, we weren't supposed to mix with children from the estate. We weren't supposed to talk about mum or look at her photos or ask any questions about her. We weren't supposed to be ill or 'make a nuisance of ourselves'. We weren't supposed to cry in front of him, even after he'd slapped us, and we were never supposed to defend ourselves or ward off his blows. We weren't supposed to tell him anything about our lives, we weren't supposed to make a fuss about doing the shopping, washing-up, mowing the lawn, hoovering, taking out the rubbish or going to the supermarket with him. We weren't supposed to tell jokes or catch each other's eye and giggle, we weren't supposed to lose our tempers with each other or tease each other or drive each other mad. We weren't supposed to talk about the outside world, our friends, school. He wouldn't tolerate the slightest draught, the slightest noise outside; the slightest laugh antagonised him, the slightest cry put his back up, two youths running down the street were always "little shits", a girl kissing some bloke was a "slut", or a "whore" if the bloke was black or Arab. Music was always by "savages" or "Negroes", television presenters were idiots, journalists traitors, civil servants layabouts, politicians thieves. Values were dying out, immigration posed a hidden threat and youth was a scourge in a world ruled by chaos. Musicians and artists were usually drug addicts, the unemployed were parasites and homosexuals were "psychopaths". Every day at four o'clock in the afternoon, my father turned on RTL and listened to the satirical radio programme *Les Grosses Têtes*. The radio came on every morning and even today, if I happen to hear the jingle for that station, a shudder of horror and disgust runs up my spine.

We weren't supposed to breathe move speak feel. We weren't supposed to need anything, pocket money or comfort or affection or smiles or advice, we weren't supposed to expect anything except the slaps, smacks or wallops he dealt out with all his strength, occasionally making do with grabbing us by the neck, wrenching our shoulders, pulling our hair and chucking us out of the house or into our bedrooms. We'd find ourselves on the floor, tears pouring down our faces, or in the frost-covered garden in winter, dressed in our pyjamas or just a T-shirt.

More often than not though, my father would begin by shouting, threatening to send us to boarding school or the army, lick us into shape and teach us what life was all about. He'd promise to give us a richly deserved beating with his belt, like his own father did when he or one of his brothers or sisters risked whispering at the dinner table. Then he'd slap us and we were supposed to remain stoical. If unfortunately we started to cry, my father would shout even louder and shower us with insults, calling us fairies and wimps, reiterating how ashamed he was of us and how much he pitied us.

My father exploded like this virtually every day, for no good reason, for a piece of paper he couldn't find, keys that had allegedly gone astray when they were in his pocket all the time, shoes lying around in the hall, a dirty mark on the tiled floor, a badly washed glass, an unmade bed, a broken flower. After punishing us, he'd leave the house and, depending on the day, would either drive off or spend hours on end in the garden chopping logs. Petrified, we'd stay in Antoine's room, listening to the sound of the car screeching off at top speed, or my father panting as he brought his axe down on the wood, the sharp, repetitive crack of the impact. Although at first we were tormented by fear, the fear that he'd injure himself with the axe or be involved in a car accident, gradually we started to hope he would die. More often than not, it was at these times that my mother chose to appear, I'd hear her voice and Antoine would suddenly look at me, or it was the other way round. We didn't need to say anything to know we'd both heard her.

I have no idea where my father went on those occasions behind the wheel of his car, the taxi sign switched off and covered with a waterproof black hood. For many years, I pictured him heading for the ring road and driving round and round Paris without taking an exit. The hoardings sped past and so did the signs, red in the car lights. A little later, I became convinced that my father visited prostitutes after one of his angry outbursts, either in Paris or at the edge of the Sénart forest, and expended his hatred between their thighs. Now I don't know any more. I just remember the feeling that time had stood still between his departure and return, the door opening suddenly, the cold air coming into the house, and his voice shouting: "I don't want to hear a peep out of you!" when we were quiet as mice, having even learnt to hold our breath, modulate and control our breathing so there was deathly silence.

A LL THIS TIME, MY BROTHER AND I were virtually inseparable. He would meet me after school, usually with Nicolas. We'd walk past areas of waste ground, squat houses with damp walls, empty bars with bored waitresses. Butchers packed with old ladies carrying shopping bags. Half-empty car parks adjacent to supermarkets with sheet-metal walls, gyms with heavily graffitied walls, playing fields with no goals or basketball boards. We'd meet up with the others at the edge of forests. The road was closed off and further on the concrete began to peter out, then there was earth, mud and ferns, clusters of trees and clearings. No one ever said anything to me, no one thought twice about my age and I liked it like that. I sat on the fence, a radio was playing the Smiths, the Cure, Lou Reed, the Clash or Nirvana, and the sub-bass thumped into the loose sandy soil. There were about ten of them, sometimes more sometimes less, as many boys as girls. The boys knocked back Bavaria 8.6 lager, tequila and gin. The girls sipped Piterson alcopops and I did the same. Joints were handed round and small pills passed from hand to hand. The girls were dressed in black with heavy make-up; some had blue, red or orange streaks in their hair. Lorette was the youngest. She was there with her sister, Laetitia, who was the spitting image of her and, from the way he stared at her, I realised that Antoine found her attractive. So did Nicolas. Lorette often sat next to me and we'd share a cigarette. Darkness fell on the rustling forest and some evenings we would light huge fires and sit around them. Some members of the group juggled, others cuddled and kissed and I watched their hands moving to and fro beneath the woollen pullovers. A few of them sneaked off, disappearing into the thickets in twos or threes, and it was never the same people. Couples formed, broke up and got back together again from one day to the next, the various configurations changing and interchanging. I followed them, sought them out in the dank undergrowth. I walked through the darkness and the ferns came up to my ankles, I crushed nettles and heather. My hands rested on tree trunks, brushed against moss sodden with rainwater. I walked blindly until I heard them groaning. I listened to the sound of their mouths, their kisses and their interlaced skin. My cock swelled fit to burst; I took it out and stroked it in the chilly darkness. I ejaculated in the bushes, the brambles and arbutus. Then I went back to the group and Lorette gave me a sidelong glance, or maybe I just felt as if people were looking at me strangely. Antoine smiled and let me have a taste of his beer. He was dancing near the fire and Laetitia got up to join him. Their eyes shone, their arms were unfolded wings, their bodies light as air, in harmony, ethereal.

Sometimes we also sat by the river. There were tiny sandy beaches dotted along the banks, straight rows of trees provided a screen. The blocks of flats opposite were a myriad of bright lights. We were joined by some fire-eaters, most of whom lived in the commune of Ris-Orangis, squatting in a disused factory where they had studios. They were waiting for darkness to fall for their acts and wore chunky sweaters rather than fireproof overalls. Flames spewed from their mouths and seemed to bounce off the wall of the air. They crouched down and tongues of fire licked the river, the water took on an orange hue then turned black and oily again. Antoine drank heavily, grabbed everything that could be smoked or swallowed. He was so out of it, he was a body dancing, a body in ecstasy. He had the fire, river, sky and night at his fingertips. The music threaded its way through each of his limbs and love flowed through his veins. He hugged us tightly in turn, exhorted us to be happy in a whisper and spoke as if he were going to die the next day. As if for him the game were already over, finished and done with. As if he'd missed the target once and for all and from now on would only place his trust in drunkenness, speed and sensation.

Those years were pack years, and Antoine acted as a sort of guide, a charismatic guardian figure for us all. It was he who decided where we would meet, who got hold of the grass, the hash, then the Ecstasy, who brought along cassettes every week that he'd recorded or stolen and that played unknown music from television and radio stations. It was he who handed out books he stole from the Gibert bookshop. Vian, Bukowski, Céline, Kerouac, Salinger. Wherever he went, I went with him, and our lives only really began once school was over for the day. I'd attend lessons like a ghost, I didn't make any friends, and sat patiently waiting for the bell. Antoine would be watching out for me near the gates. He would be chatting to Nicolas, Louis or Karim, he'd break off the minute he saw me and ruffle my hair, saying: "Let's go." We spent as little time as we could at home, running away from our father's rages and our mother's invisible yet heady presence. Real life was somewhere else and it was thrilling. Real life was curled up in Laetitia's arms and showered with Lorette's kisses.

The girls lived on the twelfth floor of a pearl-grey tower at the edge of the Youri-Gagarine estate. From their windows, you could see our house and, further away, the river and the trunk road, the artificial lake below. At night the headlamps formed chains of light or powder trails. Even further in the distance, beyond the station where the steel trains glinted, the tracks met then parted again, shaping strange itineraries. The motorway raced westwards and we gazed at it, our foreheads pressed against the cold windows. Antoine said we had to leave, take trains lorries cars, follow the lights, head for the sea, and Laetitia listened to him. She took refuge in his arms and he hugged her tightly the way we hold on to the only thing that keeps us in this world. Lorette stared at everything leaving, that network of departures, even longer, there was a crazy expression in her eyes, the blood was seething in her veins, as if something was desperate to burst out of her.

I also remember that flat in summer, Antoine and me barechested on the bed, Lorette and Laetitia wearing nothing but knickers and a camisole, our four heads touching, joined in the middle of the bed, as we lay in the shape of a star. Staring at the ceiling or eyes closed, Lorette stroked my arm. The music pounded in our heads, the grass worked its way through our lungs, our veins and with my fingertips I lightly stroked her thighs, her small breasts pearled with sweat. Our bodies moved closer, I wrapped my arms around her and my mouth searched out her mouth. She felt my erect cock against her stomach and didn't say anything, or just "hold me tight, hold me tight", like a plea.

Antoine often shouted at us to get out, to leave him alone with Laetitia. We'd turn on the television at full volume, and sometimes a record as well, but we could still hear them fucking and I could have sworn they were both crying as they did it. At those times, Lorette sat back against the wall, my head on her smooth, skinny thighs, and sucked her thumb. She looked like a little girl, which she was when I think about it. We were thirteen, fourteen or fifteen, and our eyes were bright with alcohol. Other times, we went out. I took a bottle of vodka that I slipped in my bag. We sat on a bench, the towers over our heads were gigantic shadows, darkness was falling and the windows were lighting up one by one, tiny, blurred puddles of golden light reflecting in the water. I skimmed flat stones across the surface. Lorette was shivering, she was always cold; I hugged her tight and sensed an old fear in her, a crack that nothing could ever fill. She cried or trembled even harder, black tears trickled down her cheeks, I kissed her and she bit my tongue. Antoine and Laetitia caught up with us. They were no longer walking straight and Antoine always ended up taking off his shoes, rolling his trousers up to his ankles and plunging into the murky, muddy water.

WE ALSO SPENT A GREAT DEAL OF TIME at Nicolas's place during that period. He and Antoine had met one day in a café and had become inseparable. I liked him. He was a secretive, shy, taciturn boy. He was desperately in love with Laetitia but he never breathed a word about it. His hair was long and very sleek and he wore his glasses over it so you could see the side pieces. He spent most of his time on the computer, writing complex, arcane programs that we didn't understand, and disappeared for entire weekends to take part in obscure role-playing parties. His mother was a nurse; she worked nights and when we turned up at the small house wedged at the bottom of the narrow garden, she would be asleep in her room. We hardly ever saw her, but she was kind and polite. She smoked heavily and lived on coffee. From time to time, wrapped in a threadbare cotton dressing gown, she would sit at the kitchen table and smoke a cigarette. She'd glance affectionately at us through the open door. She occasionally cooked us steaks, chips or hamburgers, or joined us when we were watching videos, the French Open or the Tour de France, slumped on the battered couch in the middle of the bare, dreary living room. On her evenings off, she would stay up with us and the M6 channel would show erotic films in which men and women in their underwear coupled on animal skins, while a saxophone played up the scene's sensuality.

Usually, though, we went down to the basement. Nicolas had a football table with bent rods, an ancient pinball machine, a makeshift drum set which he'd batter with all his might and tall stools that dated back to the time when his father owned a bar in the town centre. The bar had never done well and that town had never really had a centre. His father now worked at the Rungis market, where he unloaded pallets of flowers, meat or vegetables, depending on the day. He never came straight home, spent hours in the betting shop and if we did bump into him, he didn't make us feel welcome. He reeked of alcohol and there was a yellowish tinge to his deep-set eyes in his sharp face. He sometimes came down to the basement, watched us in silence, spat on the floor and picked up his rifle. Very slowly he would take aim at us, before leaving with a loud, chilling laugh. He would then load it and go into the garden, where he'd spend hours letting off steam by taking pot-shots at bottles. The neighbours complained about the noise but he didn't give a damn. Near the garage, he kept some rusty drums which he filled with water. Enormous catfish brought back from his fishing trips every Sunday swam around in the murk. He caught them in the Seine and left them in the drums to die. He also bred rabbits. There were loads of them huddled in cages at the rear of the property, where they shat on the straw and vacantly chewed carrots and potato peelings. I don't know what he intended to do with them. All I know is that Nicolas had to feed them and clean out their cages and he couldn't stand the creatures.

We spent so many hours, nights, days on end in the gloom of the basement. We took whole packs of beers down there, we smoked all day long, our eyes shone and our heads became hazy, anaesthetised and forgetful. Louis brought along his guitar, Alex his bass and with Nicolas as drummer they massacred 'Smells Like Teen Spirit', 'Come As You Are' or 'Hey Joe'. Lorette and Laetitia joined us, we hid in dark corners, we fucked a few feet from the others and everyone pretended not to notice. Lorette sucked me off in the dust and I took her against the cement, her hair tangled with spiders' webs. This was how time passed, we killed it, drowning it with alcohol, making it reel with music and lights, showering it with sperm and kisses.

The last time we saw him, Nicolas had shaved off his hair. His father had hit him over the head with his rifle butt. It wasn't the first time. His mother had been obliged to tend to him and stitch him up. He was wearing a dressing just above his forehead. He told us all about it in one breath, with no visible distress, very calmly, as if he were describing some minor incident. We went back to his place and he was quieter than usual. Even quieter and more impenetrable. Antoine kept glancing anxiously at him. We started playing a game of table football and I still remember the pervasive smell of cement and ivy in there, the mousetraps in the four corners of the room, the hard-earth floor and the rectangular window level with the lawn looking out over the garden, the piles of old newspapers, broken chairs, stacked tables, canvas bags hanging from hooks and filled with sand, the cracked gloves in the dust. We played listlessly, feeling choked up, and Nicolas disappeared for a few minutes. I thought he'd gone to get some beers or his music centre. He came back with the rifle. A gleam appeared in Antoine's eyes. Nicolas motioned us to follow him and the expression on his face was unreadable. We walked behind him and, outside, I was dazzled by the glare. We made for the rear of the garden. There was barbed wire along the top of the walls. In one of the drums, a dead catfish was lying on its side, just below the surface of the filthy water. Nicolas turned round and looked at us with an odd smile on his lips. He gestured towards the rabbits with his chin: "You tempted?" Antoine didn't reply and I hid behind him. Nicolas loaded the rifle, released the safety catch and fired. It took him three shots to kill the first rabbit. After that, it was a massacre. The creatures exploded dumbly and the cages were awash with blood. I went and threw up in the rose bushes. Antoine took the rifle and blew two away in his turn. Nicolas finished off the job and we returned to the basement. We drank whisky straight from the bottle to steady our nerves; Nicolas was singing at the top of his voice, I kept asking him what his father was going to say. He waved the rifle: "He'd better not kick up a stink, if he doesn't want to end up like his rabbits."

When we left the house, Nicolas was slumped despondently in the large battered armchair, his rifle on his knees. Just before we went, Antoine said to him: "Don't do anything stupid, will you?" and Nicolas replied: "Don't worry." The next day he wasn't at school. Or the next. Or ever again for that matter. I had always thought he might blow his old man away one of these days. That's what he'd said anyway. But what really happened was that he waited for him, he looked him straight in the eye, sitting in his large armchair, his head under the naked bulb hanging from the ceiling, he turned the rifle round, shoved it in his mouth and blew his own brains out.

Antoine didn't want us to go to the funeral, he didn't want to bump into Nicolas's father, he didn't want to hear the crap they'd say about Nicolas. After that, the gang broke up, that was the end of the forest fires, impromptu parties on the banks of the Seine, capricious sex in the undergrowth. Everyone stayed at home, stunned, reeling, distraught. Nicolas was dead and Antoine always said that deep down he was the only one of us with any courage and clarity. That was the saddest, blackest year with my brother. It was also the last. My father shouted at us over nothing. Mum whirled in our heads, appearing more often than ever and we were both sucked into a past with no way out. Antoine grew increasingly quiet and I was afraid. He was becoming more and more like Nicolas, I could read the same icy determination in his face, the same distress, the same madness. Laetitia was also worried. She stared sorrowfully into his eyes. She said he was drinking too much, spending too much time trying to tear himself apart, that all they did now was fuck and smoke and it was becoming tedious and depressing and morbid. My brother didn't reply; he lit a cigarette, eyes fixed on the ceiling of the flat.

It was also around this time that Lorette stopped eating. No one apart from me seemed worried that she was becoming thinner or showed any concern at her gaunt face, protruding ribs, increasingly skinny legs, her brittle torso that I no longer felt up to fondling, her almost non-existent breasts. I still wonder how she stayed on her feet. She would only drink one or two glasses of fruit juice a day, and she threw up everything I tried to get her to eat. I took her to restaurants, I cooked for her. I blew all the money I made loading and unloading crates of vegetables in the markets on Sundays on her. She forced herself to eat to please me, but at the end of the meal she invariably disappeared into the toilet and came back with red eyes and a faint reek of vomit under her Naf Naf perfume. I never talked to her mother about this. Or anyone else. I just dragged her to the doctor. I thought it was a good idea. She followed me like a zombie, she weighed less than the air at my fingertips. The surgery was carpeted in beige and decorated with abstract pictures. The doctor was a strange character; he had the appearance of an ageing ladies' man, he spoke in a fast, jerky manner, studied us with the eyes of a lunatic and, as well as the usual symptoms, wanted to know: "How have you been, otherwise?" Lorette didn't open her mouth, she was extremely weak and almost transparent. For several days, I'd felt as if she might fade away at any time. She was complaining of terrible migraines and was skipping classes to take refuge in her room, lying like a corpse in the half-light of the closed shutters, the silence of the empty flat in the middle of the afternoon. Sometimes I joined her, I slept beside her. I held her tightly as if that could keep her with me, but she was slipping away like sand through my fingers. The walls were paper-thin, but at certain times of the day we couldn't hear a thing, except the sound of our breathing. At times hers seemed about to stop and I had to listen hard.

Three days later she was staying in Brunoy, in a little clinic surrounded by trees, with red-brick walls and windows decorated with pink and orangey-yellow panes of glass. I tried to visit her on several occasions, cycling through the forest when it was muddy or fine, past comfortable houses with impeccable gardens, well-groomed lawns and teak furniture, umbrellas and dark green table-tennis tables, gleaming mountain bikes and new cars parked alongside, spaniels basking in the sun, their paws barely touching the gravel path. I left my bike leaning against the gate, walked over to reception and the lawn was strewn with large maple leaves. I searched the windows, hoping to make out her shadow at one of them. But I never saw her again. She never accepted my visits, never deigned to talk to me or even put in an appearance. I told myself that given time she'd eventually come round, that she was getting better because of the medical attention she was receiving, the treatment I knew nothing about and whose brutality I probably couldn't have imagined. But nothing happened. Laetitia passed on news to me and was worried that Lorette appeared to be remarkably happy in that establishment. She didn't seem in any great hurry to leave and, in fact, having gradually regained a more normal relationship with food, was only prevented from leaving by her panic at the outside world, which made her shake and scream with terror as soon as anyone mentioned the possibility. She stayed there for over a year. She was still there when I left my father's house. I wrote letters to her, describing the city and the life there that never stopped, the river at night, the darkness split by the garish neon lights, the constant crowds relentlessly pounding the pavements, the bars the gardens the lights, everything that bustled, that gorged itself on noise, speed, music, words and commotion. She never replied and my letters became fewer and further between. I don't know what became of her, if she's still alive, if she left her clinic. I picture her forever shut away in her room with its view of the frozen grounds, the grass burnt by frost, the bare trees against the blue sky.

THINKING BACK NOW, I realise how little I knew about Lorette. Who exactly was she? Who was I kissing all those years? Whose skinny body, with its pale veins under the skin, did I caress, penetrate, explore, turn over? I remember a shy, uncommunicative girl with a hoarse, husky voice, eyes always shining as if covered by a trembling film of water. A young girl who danced, sending arabesques of smoke spiralling from her hands. Her arms around me, my head on her shoulder, her lips around the neck of some bottle, her feet shimmying between the painted wood of the green bench and the sand below. I remember her remote expression at her bedroom window, her eyes fixed on the horizon of cement, thousands of human beings stacked together, ribbons of concrete, railway tracks, the horizon of blocks of flats and distant forests, lit windows and, unimaginable as it seemed, each one concealing thousands of monotonous, senseless lives. Lorette by the lake, walking on tiptoe, balanced on the narrow ledge, inches from the water, like a sleepwalker. Lorette at school, blowing into her recorder at full blast, producing unbearably shrill noises, bawling out 'La Chasse aux papillons' by Brassens. Lorette in art, her fingers covered with felt-tip or paint. Lorette at the start of the year, filling out her personal details and writing opposite 'Father' in black felt-tip in capital letters: 'DEAD', which he wasn't, when he'd just walked out, a long time ago, a few months after she was born, three years after Laetitia was born, walked out, to live in the vicinity or on the other side of the world, alone or with another woman, walked out without leaving a forwarding address, any note of apology or explanation, walked out in inexplicable silence, without any apparent reason, without anything to suggest he'd be back, walked out and never came back, and never again the sound of his voice on the phone, his handwriting on a letter or even a postcard. Lorette in the forest, her skin an orangey hue in the reflection of the fire, a joint in her lips and feet moving at a frantic pace, her hair iced by scattered snowflakes, swirling in the dead white sky, wetting the ground and the tree trunks, crackling softly as they died in the flames, Lorette biting my tongue with her wet teeth, and in her mouth and mine the same taste of the same blood. Lorette roaring with laughter, the strange laugh she had as of a little girl in tears, in the din of a McDonald's, around Les Halles or by the side of the trunk road, standing on the embankment of the Pont-Neuf bridge and screaming, balanced above the Seine, screaming with laughter above the barges and dark water, screaming with laughter in the large battered armchair where Nicolas waited for his father, the rifle across his knees, where he hesitated for a second when he saw him then preferred to treat the old fool to the terrifying sight of his own son eating the barrel of a rifle, his brains splattered all over the basement. Lorette shivering with cold and her tears when we fucked, her long, milky body, the deep black of her hair below her stomach, so flat then so sunken, her hair falling in curls over her tiny breasts, the sweat on her forehead, and in summer, between the pink sheets of her bedroom, the rays of light on the wall, filtered by the black plastic blinds, Lorette under the tall trees, sitting smoking on fences, by the school buildings, in her scarves, the headphones of her Walkman over her ears, Lorette at the back of cafés, Lorette crying over nothing, a sad song, someone dying in a film, three lines of a book, as if continually crying over something else that I knew nothing about. Lorette standing behind me clutching my hips on the bike along the streets lined with lime trees, past the untidy gardens with their bad-tempered dogs, pressed against me on the back of the moped, past the large lawns pitted with patches of earth and covered with dog turds, among the towers or along the river. Lorette and the miniature bottles she took everywhere, stashed in the pockets of her long black coats, her mouth and her tongue in mine and on my dick in the cinema, her hands on my stomach and chest in the heat of suburban trains, pressed up against each other at the back of a carriage, shaken about on the ripped brown leather seats covered with black marker graffiti. Lorette in the bus, her head against the window, still half-asleep, blowing her hair from her face. Lorette naked in the swimming-pool changing rooms, beckoning me over, and my tongue in her chilly, chlorinated slit. Lorette and her eyes staring at me with an expression of self-hatred or self-disgust, as she was taken by another against a tree in the dark forest, at nightfall, as the muffled pounding of the bass from the music reached our ears, as she saw me despite my hiding place in the ferns, and my eyes fixed on hers and the hand I placed on my cock. Lorette and her skin just draped over her bones, the smell of vomit at the corner of her mouth and her gaunt eyes, her cheekbones digging into me when I kiss her, and the way her whole body seems about to shatter when I squeeze her, the way you think you can crush a bird held in your hands. Lorette and her sister, leaning against each other looking out to sea, their feet in the sand. It was spring and we'd set off without a word to anyone, the four of us in the early hours of the morning, taking a detour on the way to school to catch an RER then a train at the Gare Montparnasse, getting out in Saint-Malo on a foggy morning, drinking our coffees and smoking our cigarettes at the Café de l'Ouest, smelling the nearby sea, faces and hands gnawed by the sea air, our eyes sore and our ears filled with the crash of the waves and the cries of the birds. Lorette huddled against me on the immense beach, where the rising waters met, then shoving sand into my mouth, toppling me over and kissing me, making our teeth crunch. Lorette and her sister, hand in hand, almost identical, wearing kohl under their eyes and dark lipstick, their hair dyed. Or wandering along the aisles of the supermarket, their arms round each other's hips, taking turns to kiss each other on the lips, pretending to be scandalous lesbian lovers, leaving little old men aghast, dumbfounding women with their trolleys filled to the brim with washing powder, toilet paper, meat for the freezer, pasta and sweets for the children, household products, sugar, butter and flour, detergents, socks in packs of four and corduroy slippers. Lorette looking into my eyes, mouthing a silent "I love you" that I never heard her say out loud and, immediately after, this time at the top of her voice: "I hate you, you stupid bastard, don't go getting any ideas. You just fuck me, that's all, you just kiss me, that's all." Lorette speaking in a low voice on the phone to her mother, who was the spitting image of her, a small, thin woman with dark rings under her eyes, whom we hardly ever saw, and whom she said she hated, even if I caught her being unusually affectionate on the phone. Lorette told us she worked in a bar, Laetitia said she was a cashier in a service station, and the fact that their stories didn't tie up made Antoine and me suspect they were lying, although we didn't know why. Who were they really, those unpredictable Siamese twins, who could swing from carefree laughter to black despair at a moment's notice? What do we know about the people who kiss us when we're still children? Nothing. We just kiss them back, we hold them as tightly as we can and they respond by holding us even tighter.

MY BROTHER WAS NINETEEN when he left home. I followed suit a year or more later, without asking my father's opinion, leaving him alone in his dilapidated house, its damp wallpaper peeling away in strips, garden overgrown with tall grass, poppies, nettles, mushrooms you would have thought grew in the shadow of a nuclear power station.

My brother left one night without a word. He came in and I was reading in the dark with a torch I hid under my pillow so that I could stay up late after lights out, set at eleven o'clock by my father, who was determined to "sleep in peace" undisturbed by my bedroom light, which he couldn't have seen from his room anyway. It was midnight and Antoine was dressed, his leather jacket open over his black T-shirt and a bag slung over his shoulder. I turned down the volume of my Walkman, removed my headphones. He waved to me, just said: "I'm off", and I could tell he was trying not to cry. I stood up and hugged him. I begged him for ages to tell me where he was going, if he was coming back, if he'd think of me, if he'd write to me, if I could join him one day. He gently freed himself from my embrace, smiled at me weakly and disappeared downstairs. Watching at my window, I saw him strolling unhurriedly away. I thought he'd take the last train, sleep in the streets of Paris, or on a bench near the Gare de Lyon, before going away for good, God knew where.

I didn't hear anything for three months. The telephone rang occasionally and my father picked up the receiver. I heard him repeating "Hello" and saying Antoine's name without ever getting an answer. Several times I tried to get there first, answer the phone before him. I never could.

It was in October and I was alone in the house. I heard the sound of my brother's voice and my head exploded with happiness. He was calling from Dakar, he was working in the merchant navy, his boat was on a short stopover. We hardly said a word. I was just glad to know he was alive, to be able to picture his life at sea, in ports and engine rooms. Six months later, he came back to France for a few days. He didn't come home. He arranged to meet me in Paris. I didn't really know the city, other than as a tourist, a student paying the occasional visit to the Champs-Elysées or the Les Halles district. My brother arranged to meet me in a café on the Place des Abbesses. It wasn't that long ago but the area was so different, Paris was really another city then. I waited for him by the door, I didn't dare go inside, positive that people would look at me oddly, that they'd throw me out the minute they saw me. He arrived almost at a run and his lean, tanned face stood out in contrast to the Parisians' late winter pallor. Antoine had changed. His face had aged years in a few months, he had filled out, his face was hidden behind a bushy beard and his eyes were bulging out of his sockets. With his close-cropped hair, right arm covered with tattoos, I was no longer sure I'd ever really known him.

We went into the café and I sat down opposite him. The radio was playing old Doors songs, he ordered a beer and asked how I was. I answered vaguely. I gazed intently at him. He'd changed so much. I swallowed a mouthful of beer. We were surrounded by groups of students who looked nothing like us and seemed to belong to a different species, a protected species. They were wearing velvet jackets and scarves and had shoulder-length hair, boys as well as girls. They had elegant mannerisms, smoked affectedly, laughed without being vulgar and talked about music, films and literature.

Feeling lost in the midst of all this, my brother and I looked at each other—we were alone in the world, cut-off, permanently on another planet. Antoine ordered another beer, I asked him about his life, but he had nothing to say about it. He worked on a boat, he spent weeks at sea, in the middle of nowhere, docked in foreign towns where he only saw the port, the quays where they loaded or unloaded merchandise. He did some shopping, sometimes had a drink in a bar, then it was time to leave again. The rest of the time he worked, slept, and that was that. It was a physical, mind-numbing life, reeling with wind and weariness, sleepless nights and nights when he slept like a log, cigarettes, card games, alcohol, and there was nothing else to say. "Anyway, what about you? How's it going?" He didn't ask about our father, and it was better that way.

When it came down to it, my brother and I had never really spoken to each other. We'd never had a *conversation*. We had nothing to tell each other, nothing to prove, we loved each other with a boundless love and that was that. The only thing we should have done that day was hug each other but we didn't dare. Before he left, he just told me, eyes gazing into space and teeth clenched, that wherever he went, he was haunted by my father's voice, that it didn't matter how many thousands of miles he travelled, or if he disappeared off the face of the earth, our father's icy, infuriated voice, the perpetual threat of his rage, would stay with him and choke him, would knot his stomach and make him long for death without knowing why.

We strolled through the streets for a while, everything bathed in the artificial light of streetlamps and neon signs. Near the Place Blanche, Antoine pointed out the hotel where he was staying the night. It was a grotty building, its peeling walls flushed red by the glow of nearby signs. Before turning in, he was going to hang around in some bars, listen to some music, have a few drinks and, he volunteered with a half-smile, hopefully he wouldn't come back alone. I left him standing there, I came back a few times, I was turning into the Rue Fontaine when I saw him go into one of the peep-shows for tourists near the Moulin Rouge. I walked up steep streets, blinded by tears, my brother and I had failed each other, and this would happen virtually every time.

I DON'T REMEMBER WHEN we last got together. I was living with Claire and my first book had just been published or was about to be. It was in Marseilles, he'd phoned me two months earlier to let me know, I'd made the trip just to see him and it was the last time. How many years is it since I've heard from him? Five, perhaps. A little less, a little more, I don't remember. My brother has been lost at sea, so to speak. I often take the motorbike, leave the outskirts of Douarnenez and drive to Brest. I spend hours wandering around the commercial port among the cranes, vast warehouses, tiny bars where people drink standing up, a cigarette clamped between their teeth, gazing at machines manipulating enormous pallets, containers swinging in the air before coming to rest on the quays. I watch the men working there, I examine the ones who stay on deck, I wander round the showers, canteens, minimarkets where they stock up on razor blades, toothpaste, soap, deodorant, chocolate bars, flasks of alcohol, newspapers of all kinds, biscuits, cigarettes. I search their tanned, prematurely wrinkled faces, their cracked skin, I search their lean bodies for the frail silhouette of my runaway brother. But my heart has never started beating faster in my chest thinking I've seen him. Never. My brother has disappeared and, deep down, from year to year, from meeting to meeting, from stopover to stopover, this is what he seemed to be doing. Every time, I recognised him a little less, his old gestures were superseded by new ones; his smiles, his mannerisms, his face were replaced by other smiles, other mannerisms, another face. My brother was changing, the way someone wipes the slate clean, makes a fresh start, and soon, in this irreversible process, I was the last vestige of a past life, a life he wanted to forget.

The telephone rang and it was the middle of the night. He just said: "It's me." Claire groaned, rolled over several times in her sleep and murmured groggily: "Who is it?" I stumbled out of the bedroom, the receiver clamped to my ear. From his breathing, his silence, I could tell he had a catch in his throat and that he'd been drinking. I asked him where he was and as always he replied: "On the other side of the world, where do you think?" It was ten months since I'd seen him. The last time was in Brest, I'd met up with him and we'd spent the night drinking in the Recouvrance district. In the morning, the boat set sail again for Egypt, Chile, New York and Finland.

He was calling me from a bar in Australia. Over there, guys would drink lager by the litre, never less. That afternoon, he'd rented a four-wheel drive and gone out for a drive for a change and had knocked down three kangaroos. He missed me, that's what he told me, and also that I was his favourite kid brother and I could almost feel his hand tousling my hair. He asked if I had any news. There was nothing special I wanted to tell him. I just wanted him to carry on speaking, I just wanted to hear his voice and fall asleep with it. Hear him tell me he was close by. Tell me that he was happy and things were okay. He went on and soon the words were pouring out in a rambling flood, he was crying and swallowing half his words. He told me about a girl and how badly she'd hurt him, about the fever that had laid him low for two weeks. About Laetitia whom he missed, about mum and her face when she was dead. In his mind's eye, she still looked like that, never any different, her face bony and powdered, her eyelids shut. About her voice which he'd forgotten. The softness of her neck when he would kiss her there as a boy.

"When are you coming back?"

"In two months. I'll be in Marseilles."

"Tell me, Antoine, was papa always like that?"

"What are you talking about?"

"Was he always like that or did it start when mum died? I don't remember. I don't remember him before that. I can't remember how he was with us, if he acted as if he loved us a bit or what?"

My brother didn't reply. When he hung up, I cried myself silly in the living room. Through the window, I could see the building opposite, the cracked walls and, lower down, the dark paving slabs where sickly plants were dying.

Two months later, I took a day's holiday and the train to Marseilles. I waited for him in a café in the *Vieux Port* filled with people talking at the top of their voices. It smelled of beer, pastis, and there were footballers dashing about on the giant screen. He arrived with his bag over his shoulder, his cigarette between his lips. He said: "Let's get out of here," and we wandered aimlessly through the streets of the Panier district. At times, without warning, the dazzling horizon appeared, the sea stretched out at our feet, heaving with iron-grey freighters, between the dingy, orange walls. We rented a room and the hotel had a view of the Calanques. It was very noisy, there were people shouting in the streets and Arab or African music on the beach. The windows were wide open. The blades of a ceiling fan revolved sluggishly. Lying side by side on the mauve sheet, the air caressed our skin. We fell silent to listen to the sea. He said it didn't sound the same in other places. The sea sounded different in every single place he stopped. I don't remember what we talked about. All I know is that we were hot and I could feel the sweat from his arm on mine, that our skin stuck together in places and that I would have liked to stay like that forever. At dawn, we walked to the beach and he went skinny-dipping as the sun was coming up. He showed me his new tattoos on his back and chest; I told him I liked them. He had that faint smile, the one I'd always loved, the one he wore when he knew he was impressing me. Suddenly my mother started to float on the still water, then dissolved after barely a second.

I never saw or heard from him again after that. I don't know if he's still living that life, if he finally settled down somewhere, or if he's dead.

AFTER ANTOINE LEFT, I was on my own with my father for several months. During that time, he worked less, spent most of his time in the house, hardly ever went out, not even into the garden that he had eventually allowed to run riot. He killed the days in front of the television or reading motor magazines from cover to cover. We ate our meals separately and I stayed in the house as little as possible, or shut myself in my room. We only saw each other briefly and, for some absurd reason, I lived in dread of him coming into my room, armed with a baseball bat or a lump of wood, and silently starting to beat me until I lost consciousness.

The year I turned seventeen, I left the house without a word. After I left, like my brother, I didn't get in touch with my father and I don't think he ever tried to get in touch with me. I didn't see him until a year later and that was the last time we met. It was summer and I was earning a living as a nightwatchman in the Strasbourg-Saint-Denis district. The guests at the hotel were immigrants who worked mainly in the evenings and slept during the day. While they were out, we rented their rooms to Albanian, African or Chinese prostitutes who worked along the Boulevard de Strasbourg. For some reason, I was obsessed with the idea that one day I'd see my father turn up on the arm of one of these women, that I'd have to look him in the face, greet him and collect the one hundred and fifty francs that he'd hand over, pretending either that he hadn't recognised me or that he'd completely forgotten who I was. It never happened though. I simply bumped into him one evening on my way to work, in a nearby bar that was one of my regular haunts. He was drinking a beer, his face was thin and he was watching the horse-racing on a television set. He was wearing a cap, baggy trousers too big for him and he seemed terribly frail and old. Seeing him like that, so tiny and insignificant, I wondered for a second how my brother and I could have been so afraid of him. I ordered a coffee, standing among the sugar wrappers, fag ends and betting slips. In the murky light, the races were being run one after the other and the punters were filling out their tickets on the yellow Formica tables. From time to time, they looked up, brought their glasses to their lips, and watched the horses chasing round the track. Some were jumping fences, others didn't make it, sprawling flat in the mud and crushing their pint-sized jockeys. The owner nodded to me by way of a greeting and, wiping his hands on his black apron, came out with his usual: "So, Monsieur Olivier, how are you this evening?" My father didn't turn round at my name, but after all that was probably only natural, there are loads of blokes with my name, even though of course I jump every time I hear someone say my mother's name or call out Chloé, Antoine or Lorette, even at the cinema, even on television. I went over to him, I put my hand on his shoulder, it was the first time I'd touched him like that. He turned round and his face was completely expressionless. "How're things? How're you doing?" That was all he said. Then, without waiting for a reply, he turned back to the television. I paid for my coffee and left. I remember it was raining and the sky was so black that it seemed as if darkness had fallen already, even though it was still two hours before nightfall.

I don't know anything about my father. I don't have any memories of him in the three years leading up to my mother's death. And the rest is pitch dark. I know nothing about him, but I can't help dreaming that he was a different man then, that he talked to us, kissed us, smiled at us, made time to play with us, go for bike rides, took us to football practice or just checked our homework. I dream about it but I don't remember anything. He never said anything about himself, never told me anything about his childhood, how he met my mother, the jobs he did before he started working as an independent taxi driver, how he paid for his licence plate, how old he was when he began, if he'd studied before that, if he'd worked when he was young or not. All I know is that he lived with his brothers and sisters in a two-bedroom flat in Clamart, that he was one of the youngest and that his father wouldn't stand for any talking at the meal table. I only have a few photos of him. One in military service, a cigarette in his mouth and his cheek against his Famas rifle, another in class at the age of ten, an impeccable left-hand parting, an ironed checked shirt barely visible under his school smock, a strained smile for the occasion, and that's about it. Then there are the photos of my mother and they are from before Antoine was born. The colour of mum's hair is different in every one of these, as are her dresses. As for my father, he only makes a rare appearance, usually striking a conspicuous pose, a slight smile on his lips, sometimes acting the clown, looking relaxed and likeable. In a few, he's holding my mother round the waist, they are walking or he is kissing her, or they are both roaring with laughter, him wearing only a pair of shorts and her in a swimsuit, a scarf in her hair at the wheel of a Citroën DS or stretched out on a lounger on the terrace of a holiday home in Lot or the Pyrenees. These photos are proof. They are all I have to go on. These photos are the only evidence I possess that my father could be tender, warm, loving, even humane.

III

IN THE OPEN

I'VE GONE OUT, leaving Claire and Chloé deep in their angelic sleep. The night is gradually giving out. The promenade is deserted, frosted by an icy wind. I pass shadows, wind-battered bodies, invisible faces. I walk beside hotels with dark windows, bars with stacked tables. I hear a child crying and my heart turns over.

At the end of the strip of cement, a staircase disappears into the darkness and visibility decreases with every step I take. To the right, a few yards from the cliffs, leaving the dark sand and grey pebbles exposed, the sea flexes like a muscle, fills the air, and seems the whole world. I'm following in my mother's footsteps, walking like her through the deep darkness, my lungs filling with wind and the raw aroma of the water. I'm following her tracks and my memory is like the sky streaked with the progress of charcoal clouds, my childhood buried under how many pounds of sand?

I'm following in my mother's footsteps, I'm walking towards her death, several times I fall over and my knees are covered with loose soil, mud works its way into my palms, pebbles crunch beneath them. It doesn't take long to reach the top of the cliffs, they curve and break for miles. I can't see a thing and the wind presses me back, makes my head spin and my eyes sting. I walk to the very edge, I could close my eyes and try to guess where the land ends, take that one extra step that would slam me against the sand, dismembered, mangled, smashed to pieces hundreds of feet below.

I'm following in my mother's footsteps, I hear her voice, she's right in front of me, alive and light, her face haggard under her long hair. Suddenly she disappears. Several birds fly past and I'd swear their wings brush against me, they call and I answer them. I know there aren't many of them, but there are thousands round me, they keep me company in a strident cortège. Gulls—great and lesser black-backed, common, herring and slender-billed, black-headed or Bonaparte's—plovers, terns—roseate, Caspian, bridled and lesser-crested—herons, little auks, rock birds, common murres, northern gannets, cormorants, British storm petrels, shearwaters, northern fulmars and Eurasian oystercatchers endlessly circle the cliffs with their unfamiliar outlines, I don't know where they start and where they end.

Everything is whistling around me, I'm becoming one with the wind, the roar of the sea, the wheeling of the birds, I'm an empty body dissolving in the darkness. I stumble and my cheek scrapes against the dry moor, hardened by the cold. I feel a trickle of warm blood on my forehead. The gulls are coming to eat my eyes I think, the night is spinning, so are the moon and stars. I scream, as if to purge everything, but my voice is lost in the gusts of wind and the roaring of the Channel and I can barely hear it. I'm a black night, a cliff edge, a life lost at sea, with a view of the sheer drop and no fear of heights.

We left Paris the way people run to save their skin. We put an end to my zombie-like existence, the pathetic, despondent hours of living death, whittled away by alcohol. The house is a stone's throw from the cliffs and a crescent of beach. The peninsula stretches out into the sea a long way, the moor adopts thousands of colours, overrun by mulberry bushes, moss and heather, Crozon smells of fern, damp rock and liquorice. In the early days, Claire mocked my fondness for birds; I could spend hours watching them, their strange flight paths, sudden turns and luminous curves. Claire would leave in the morning and I'd drink my coffee in the harbour, revelling in the sluiced light, the changing skies. Trawlers were returning from the open sea, unloading glistening crates of silvery fish and spreading nets out to dry on the quays. Afterwards I'd drive my motorbike along miles of headlands and inlets, stop to plunge my hands in the sand, near the ornithological centre. Along the road, the windmills turned slowly and the rock was grey and green. Several bleak villages were perched on the edge, walls made of thick, dark stone, their inhabitants hewn by the wind. I spent hours in the area around the centre, watching the enclosures where they tended injured cormorants, keeping a close eye on the secretive activity of people who devoted their life to counting birds, to taking a census of the different species.

This way of life didn't cure me of anything, it was merely possible when I couldn't cope with any other kind of life, particularly the one I'd just left behind. It was a life of silence, space and absence, of maintaining an acute presence within objects, the shifting play of light, the still motion of water, the perfumes, the texture of the air. It was a life in which I finally found a niche, quiet but peaceful, a body filled with air and fog, a mind completely given over to the noise of the sea and wind, the company of birds. I wrote sometimes. In the damp evenings, Claire would lavish kisses on me and we'd drink late into the night, while everything creaked in the house, while the trees reeled and the world cracked open behind our closed shutters. Then it was summer and I found a job on a beach as a waiter in a seasonal straw hut with a bamboo roof. Children covered themselves in icing sugar, old men sipped Perrier and lemon tea, the younger men drank beers, devoured panini or waffles, then headed back into the water, half-naked or clad in black wetsuits. All day, I had the sea in front of me, I watched the tide coming in and going out, the sun reflecting on the damp sand pocked with small basins, where toddlers paddled. There were two of us manning the place and we took it in turns to sleep there overnight. I would lock the shack and spread a makeshift mattress on the floor. A baseball bat within easy reach, a mace spray in my jacket pocket, wrapped up warmly in three blankets, I'd listen to the tide coming in and it sometimes felt as if the water were so close that it would soon flood the place and engulf me. I went out every now and then and the boats rocked in the moonlight, the lines of rocks were tiny islands perched with sleeping gulls. I stripped off and dropped my clothes on the sodden sand, the nights were sometimes very mild and the perfectly calm sea lapped around my ankles, then my thighs and whole body, I walked with my feet completely flat, slowly going deeper and deeper, until my nostrils were level with the surface. My body was frozen, I couldn't feel anything any more, my mind was completely liquid and the moon painted bright, blurred lines on the dark surface. Claire sometimes joined me and we slept side by side in the absolute darkness of our wooden surroundings, the murmur muffled but still enveloping everything, lulling us, encompassing us.

The years flew past like that. I spent the autumn and winter travelling the length and breadth of the coast, getting high on wind, losing myself on paths, chewing grass and sleeping in the rocks, drinking whisky as the air rasped against my skin, writing books that would be published six months later. Then the new season began and I went back to my shelter on the beach, my starry nights, my turns of guard duty when nothing ever happened. Occasionally, lads climbed on the roof, couples broke into the beach huts and sheltered there to fuck, teenagers showed up in the evening, stayed until closing time, then wandered off over the sand, juggled with fiery torches, filled the night with the noise of djembe drums, smoked joints around a fire, groped each other under thick woollen blankets, kissed full on the mouth and skinny-dipped. Only once did I have to use my bat, only once did I see wooden planks lifting with the splintering sound of crowbars wedged in and bolts snapping. Before I was hired, there had been a few attempted thefts; one had landed my predecessor in the hospital with a broken nose after being beaten as he tried to save sandwiches, drinks, frozen chips, coffee machines and waffle irons. The thieves came in through the windows and I stood there waiting for them in the darkness. I only had to hit out once, at random. My bat smashed into a face or something, bones cracked, there was a scream and they ran off. I spent the night repairing the damage.

I like this life of family summers, packed beaches, mechanical gestures and smiles. I like the fact that everyone seems happy and relaxed, that financial directors and aggressive slave-drivers end up scantily dressed as they play ball or build castles that will be demolished in the blink of an eye by the tide or the kids. In the mornings, I like seeing families bending over the sand, hunting for molluscs, the kids kitted out with shrimping nets and wellies. In the golden light then growing darkness of evening, I like seeing couples, young or old, holding hands and walking along the smooth, shining sand, smoking cigarettes, gazing up at the sky, strolling and gesticulating, elegantly holding forth and smiling in a way that would be impossible anywhere else. I like the evenings of fireworks, the overcrowded beach and the kids with their lanterns, the bangers and the jostling crowd waiting to be served. I like the wan mornings and the beach abandoned to the birds, and the bloke paid by the tourist office who comes here to play the bagpipes, standing in the sea. I serve him until noon with glasses of white wine that he drinks as he comments on current events.

I liked that summer, it was the third, a few months before Claire fell pregnant. There were about ten of them, all related to varying degrees, who would turn up around nightfall. They were between twelve and sixteen, they would order coffees and beers that I served with a knowing wink, and sit near the Club Mickey, recognisable in the evening by its four pale wooden fences and the slides mobbed by children on their way back from their walks. She kept herself to herself, always wore black jumpers which she pulled up over her chin and were too heavy for the season. She was fifteen or sixteen with very straight jet-black hair. She was a strange, surly girl, unreadable and shy. She threw me dark, intense glances, her small face extremely serious and mesmerising. She'd come up with her heavily made-up eyes, thin lips, just before closing time. I'd buy her a few drinks and she'd sigh watching the others, who irritated her intensely. She was there for a month, staying with her grandmother, whom she escaped in the evenings. The old lady went to bed very early and, with time, I'd gradually learnt to pick out her and her grandmother amongst the sunbathers, always in the same spot. The old lady did crossword puzzles between two swims, while the girl never took off her sunglasses or T-shirt. She slowly acquired the habit of spending time with me, of sharing my shelter. She liked its shipwrecked feel and would whisper things to me. Her father was dead and it was only a few months ago, a stupid accident but what difference did that make, he was dead and something about my face or my eyes reminded her of him a little. I listened to her and looking like a dead man didn't matter at all to me. She told me in whispers about her humdrum days, about absence and feeling bogged down, her indifference to other people, the way she always felt as if there were a thick pane of glass, a translucent wall of cotton wool, a curtain of rain, between her and the world. She told me about the hours spent in cafés and her interminable classes, the sun on her skin and the music that made her forget herself, the way her father appeared and smiled at her before vanishing without a trace. There was an age gap of thirteen years between us but we were so alike. Not that I told her that. I was happy to guard her succession of confidences and her age-old assortment of mundane sorrows. I sometimes wonder why she chose me, so to speak, what it was about my attitude, my gestures or my face that gave me away, if it was all part of some kind of instinctive recognition that sometimes brings birds of a feather together and, especially, perhaps even more than the rest, those that are most fragile and least well-equipped to brave the cold winds. One day she admitted that I was convenient for her, that I was a grave in which she could bury her secrets, that my presence was so tenuous, so intangible, that someone could endlessly fill me up and make me anything they wanted. In the wavering light of a torch, she removed her pullover and her breasts pierced the darkness. We made love under the roar of the waves, I shut my eyes and it felt as if I were kissing Lorette again, her small, bony body, her narrow hips and tiny breasts. She stared at me and gritted her teeth; there were times I thought I was hurting her. Then she fell asleep against me, and she fitted in my hand, suddenly no bigger than a child. This went on for about three weeks and then she left. Sometimes she made fun of me, laughingly calling me a pervert, wanted to know if my wife knew I was sleeping with minors. I didn't say anything in reply, I just shrugged, I didn't know my own age, my life was so small and I'd seen so little, I was just a child, I was eleven and my mother was dead, the world was bitterly cold and I was shivering, I needed someone to put their arms around me and comfort me, to rock me and warm me up a little. Exactly like her.

My feet stumble on pebbles or sink into the cold, spongy moss. The world is reduced to a mass of sharp, whistling noises, layers of black and grey, displaced air and my outer shell covers nothing, contains nothing. I could die just as easily. Like my mother I could die and my eyes fill up with tears and like her I walk towards the sheer drop and Chloé's face floats under my eyelids and in my head, and I wonder if she too, as she was dying or was about to die, saw our faces, mine and Antoine's, projected against the dark screen of the sea and sky combined. I collapse, the soaked grass welcomes me and serves as a chilly bed. I couldn't die as easily as her, I know. Never. Chloé has been born and I know now that I'll never be able to die. And I prefer not to realise that I'd also been born and that didn't prevent anything.

IT WAS SUMMER WHEN I TURNED UP at the Gare du Nord with my shoulder bag and a few savings. I recall walking aimlessly through the stifling, crowded streets, jostled by thousands of sweaty bodies, walking past stalls piled high with meat, tons of vegetables and exotic fruit sticky with juice. I remember the dirty cafés where men played draughts, shops filled with all kinds of junk, call shops where people spoke every language under the sun and Asians and Africans sat waiting their turn in front of rows of open booths to be connected to Sudan, Senegal, Thailand, Iran or Morocco. Hotels with dilapidated facades and grimy paintwork stood in similar streets. Men were hanging around outside, mainly black, on the lookout for something, yelling into their mobiles or shouting at each other across the street, roaring with laughter. It was Paris but it didn't look like it or, at least, that's what I thought then, before I realised that Paris didn't look like itself any more, and that this was the only way you could love it, before I even realised that Paris was now like nowhere else on earth. A city of museums, a city of offices, a city of luxury boutiques and interior design shops, unaffordable restaurants, a city for 'fooding', shopping, clubbing, well-off couples who save and invest, property-owners and professionals. I rented a room in a hotel. The walls were very tatty, the wallpaper was peeling away in entire strips or was full of holes where the damp had eaten through. The paintwork was coming off, revealing the crumbling cement walls beneath. Whole families lived, slept and watched television there, six of them eating together in those cramped rooms. All the doors were open and people were chatting from one room to another, different musics blared out at full volume, intermingling and drowning each other in a strange hubbub, kids raced along the corridors and pelted up and down stairs dressed only in pants or football shorts. I put my bag down and the cockroaches ran for cover under the sagging bed. The room had a poor-quality mattress, a cupboard and a mirror above the chipped china sink. A few days later, I started work as a watchman at a hotel that was just like it in every respect.

I stayed in this hotel for about ten days, the time it took to find a job, open a bank account, rent a room. I didn't go out much, the heat was stifling and I lay there virtually naked, my sheets drenched with sweat. I would doze until the evening when it turned a little cooler; I scoured the district and the bars, I came back late and the hotel was even less restful at night. There was loud music playing and everyone was shouting, laughing, fighting. Every three minutes, someone knocked on my door and invited me in for a drink. It was hard to resist and I soon found myself in the middle of a tiny room where fat women were cooking meat on portable stoves. Young girls wearing incredibly tight jeans and multicoloured braided hair extensions were chattering non-stop in shrill voices. People were knocking back punch, whisky straight from the bottle and bottles of beer while leaning out of the window. The children eventually fell asleep in a corner on a mattress, a balled-up jacket or on the floor. Joints were being passed round in double-quick time, the men clicked their tongues and some of them occasionally began extravagant speeches in English about love, brotherhood, the Lord, Africa and France. The rest agreed, clapped their hands or yelled "amen" at every sentence. On the fourth evening, one girl didn't take her eyes off me, she danced and I could tell it was all for me, her pert arse swayed right under my nose, she held out her hands to me and I did my best, I didn't have to do much, she was tall and perfumed, her skin was dark and glistening, she rubbed her buttocks against my cock and laughed when she felt my erection. We left the room, she turned to me in the corridor with its crackling light bulbs, gave me the come-on with warm, hungry looks, winks and lewd gestures. In my room she continued to dance as she undressed. Then she came close, touched my face with her fingertips, saying: "You've got lovely eyes, you've got lovely lips." She pulled off my T-shirt and kissed me tenderly or bit me. She took my cock in her mouth and we fucked standing up, my stomach sometimes brushed her back, my hands clasped her breasts, her hands placed flat against the wall. Then we slept and I don't think she released my prick once during all that time, she held it in her hands like a bird, sometimes squeezing it gently, waking me up. The minute I touched her arse I was hard again and a moist dance began and her voice was husky, you'd have sworn she was singing when she came. Day dawned and I had an appointment near Les Halles, a café was looking for a waiter, one of the Africans at the hotel had told me about it the day before, he'd tried his luck but had got nowhere, obviously. The café owner greeted me, it was early and we both had a glass of white wine, then another for the road, and a third to celebrate my new job. I returned to the hotel in a rainstorm, soaked to the skin and the air was still as heavy and humid. The hotel was strangely quiet. All the doors were open and the rooms were empty or trashed, ripped mattresses spewing an orangey-yellow foam over the floor, scattered piles of clothes, broken bottles and bloodstains. My room had been ransacked, the entire contents of my bag spread over the tiled floor, sheets rumpled and the mattress overturned. I sensed someone behind me, I turned round and it was the guy from reception, a pale, sickly man whose open shirt revealed an incredible collection of scars, and who had a gun hidden in his drawer.

He'd showed it to me one evening, it was a heavy, gleaming weapon and I'd made a mental note it was there, in case I needed it one day.

"The police turned up. They carted everyone away. Not one of them had valid papers. They're sending them home on a chartered flight."

"That's disgusting," I said. "The police are pigs."

"It's not disgusting at all, young man, it's the law, and they just enforce it. As for the rest, believe me, they just want to earn a crust and enjoy a peaceful weekend at home with the wife and kids. Like you and me. Anyway, those people have no right to be here."

"But they do have the right to give you their cash, don't they?"

"Oh, come off it. If it wasn't me, it'd be someone else. And anyway it was high time those people got the hell out of here, I haven't had a penny from them for ten days."

I told him I wanted to be alone and he walked off with a sigh. I didn't want to think about it, picture her in the hands of the police, the detention centre, the charter planes and the handcuffs, I didn't want to think about the fear, the children, the truncheon blows, the twisted arms, the babies crying. The next day, all the rooms were taken by Africans no more or less legitimate than the previous occupants, but most of them had enough to pay for a few nights at least.

After that, I moved to a room under the eaves, near the Ternes district. I paid a derisory rent in cash to a tall man with an aristocratic sounding 'de' to his name, who lived three floors down and looked like Valéry Giscard d'Estaing. He looked at me somewhat askance and every month would stand in the doorway of the tradesman's entrance. Behind him, I imagined a series of immense sitting rooms with dark carpets, cluttered with large armchairs upholstered in bottle-green or burgundy velvet, walls hung with hunting scenes, copies of Flemish paintings and originals by minor artists. I reached my room via a dirty, narrow staircase that seemed out of place in a building like this. The toilet was on the landing and the room was tiny, with a chest of drawers, a bed and a table I used as a desk and on top of which I stood a portable gas stove. The window in the sloping ceiling, on which I'd bang my head when I woke with a start from one of those dreams where mum appeared and beckoned to me (so I'd make my way towards her and, as I came nearer, she'd back away, her face blurring until her features vanished), overlooked the Alexander Nevsky cathedral. I spent hours with my forehead pressed against the glass gazing at its gilded Christ and the bare trees surrounding it in winter, the funerals three times a week. In the early days, I hung a birdcage outside the window as a cooler where I kept butter, yoghurt, and meat, when I happened to buy it, which actually wasn't very often. I lived on pasta, rice, semolina, fruit and cheap wine, which I drank in astronomical quantities and which took the edge off my hunger enough for me to skip most meals. I remember the rough, grey fitted carpet and the stains spattered over it, like islands in the middle of the sea, an imaginary cartography whose outline I think I could recreate today. The ribbons of dust that descended onto it on sunny mornings. The saggy bed with the broken legs I replaced with red bricks I found in the street. The lurching walls and the strange plastic shower stall, close to the cracked basin, and higher up the ramshackle window, overlooking the wall and the light well. There were five similar rooms along the corridor. One of the tenants didn't have running water and would use the tap near the toilet to fill up bowls, do his laundry and have a wash early in the morning or in the middle of the afternoon, when he thought he was alone on the floor. He was a man of about fifty, a Serb with an angular face hesitantly covered by a straggly grey beard. He occupied the room at the end and carried out small wiring, plumbing, painting and gardening jobs for the local Orthodox community. I occasionally bumped into him in the street, sweeping the square in front of the cathedral, repainting the front of the restaurant adorned with Russian dolls and red and black tablecloths, where blonde chanteuses with heavily rouged cheeks sang in the evenings, accompanied by violinists with missing teeth. Often at night, around three or four in the morning, I'd hear him struggling up the six flights of stairs to reach his flat, roaring drunk and armed with bottles. He'd trip over with a dull, heavy thud accompanied by the sound of glass banging against the steps. He seemed to take hours to get upstairs and the nearer he came, the clearer I could hear his hoarse breathing and the oaths he muttered in his own language. Once he was home in one piece, out of breath and staggering, he would stop in the corridor, speak out loud and take a long pee in the toilet. The noise his urine made in the water of the toilet bowl filled the quiet night. The songs he sang wildly in a deep voice occasionally drowned out this noise. From time to time, I paid him a visit in his tiny room and the floor was strewn with empty bottles. With his back to me, he'd rummage for ages in large plastic bags from which he'd eventually take out the joint or hash balls I'd come to cadge off him. He regularly came over to my place for coffee, on the scrounge for bread or a bar of soap, or to repair a leak for which he never accepted any payment. He invariably went into raptures over the size of my room, which was only about ten square metres and at least a third of that space had a sloping ceiling. I spent most of my time sitting on the floor. He'd finger my books without opening them, ferret around in my records and sometimes ask me to play one, merely on the strength of its cover. He'd listen, eyes reverently closed, to songs by Nick Drake, Bob Dylan or Leonard Cohen that filled the room. He liked me to turn up the volume so that the music drowned out everything. My next-door neighbour, a paranoid elderly Spanish woman, would start to scream, coming out of her flat to call me a savage, order me to stop that God-awful racket and threaten to call the police. She never did and, anyway, I think she feared them like the plague. Bumping into her on the ground floor when I was picking up my post, she'd occasionally tell me in confidence that her post was systematically stolen or, rather, held back at source, checked, opened, violated, by order of the highest state authorities. She claimed she knew too much about various subjects, all of which came within the remit of a vague conspiracy theory. In her gloomy flat, with its furniture covered with black, openwork doilies and its walls plastered with crucifixes, portraits of the Madonna and painted plates from Lourdes, Jacques Chirac smiled out from a gilt frame next to Pope John Paul II. She claimed she knew both men personally. She was totally unpredictable, and I never knew, when walking past her door, if she was going to open it and accuse me of a thousand criminal acts (the worst was pulling the chain in the middle of the night, since the communal toilet was next to her room, and she herself never used it, making use instead, she told me one day, of a plastic bowl that she insisted on showing me, and in which I had on several occasions seen her doing her laundry), or if she would invite me in, insist on offering me tea and soft, soggy biscuits that she took from ornamental iron boxes, and regale me under the seal of secrecy with the private affairs of the Pope and the mayor of Paris.

I lived in that room for four years and I watched my Serbian neighbour disintegrating daily: his teeth and skin turned yellow, dark rings took up permanent residence under his eyes, his nose got rounder and redder with pores like gullies and his smell turned sour. I watched his conversation dry up, his loud laughter and drunken songs tail away, choked off by a cough that soon became his constant companion. In the end, he was almost mute and only ever left his room to take a pee or fetch water from the tap.

My room in the middle of the corridor was flanked by two other rooms. The one on the left was occupied by a fat Russian man of about forty, a waiter in a nearby restaurant, who, because of my service record in the restaurant business, only ever called me "colleague". He came back from work at the dead of night and when I was at home, I could hear him take a shower, turn on the television and begin snoring half an hour later. He got up around midday and spent the afternoon in his flat, dressed in a burgundy dressing gown that he only took off in the evenings to don his elegant black waiter's uniform, his hair slicked back and his freshly-shaved cheeks glowing red. I'd bump into him in the corridor or he'd knock on my door. At the weekend, we lived the same life, working all or part of the night and sleeping during the day, dozing in the afternoon, wandering around in a fog of tiredness. He would sometimes invite me in for a drink and his home was incredible, stinking of alcohol and semen, sweat and cold tobacco. The walls were plastered with photos of naked women spreading their legs to reveal pink, red or bright purple shaved pussies. The television set was always switched on, showing grey, grainy images of Russian videos, miles of low-budget, over-written, hammed-up serials, bizarre clips of musicians in military dress confidently faking Depeche Mode, AC/DC or Guns N' Roses in their own language. He sat on his leather couch and left me the armchair, his dressing gown gaped open over his podgy, hairless torso, his baggy pants displayed a glimpse of one ball. He served me large measures of vodka or whisky that I knocked back without turning a hair. Regularly, as he sat there glued to the screen, he yelled at me to look, going into raptures over the beauty of a singer or actress whom he invariably dreamt of screwing. We drank without saying a great deal; I suppose he enjoyed my company. Also, fairly often, he would come looking for me in my room and take me back to his place, where two whores would be waiting for us. Always blonde, dressed in fur coats, wearing too much make-up and dripping with heavy gold jewellery, they barely spoke French and always ended up on our laps unbuttoning our shirts. They would then suck us off on their knees, their blouses open over their heavy breasts. He usually went no further than that, helped the girl up and embraced her with his eyes closed, cheek to cheek, in a suddenly sexless act of tenderness, as if cuddling a child or allowing himself to be comforted by his own mother. As for me, I'd take myself off with my partner, regain the modesty of my room and fuck her in the intense light generated by the sun at that hour of the afternoon.

As time went by, he had fewer and fewer visits from whores and towards the end, when I bumped into him and he invited me to follow him, he would walk wearily to his room and collapse on the couch. He'd light a cigar, take a swig of vodka from the bottle and soon doze off while I watched the television, which was now showing endless scenes of fellatio, cunnilingus and double penetration imported from Eastern Europe. I remember that the images ran into one another and had no more effect on me than an animal documentary. The last time I saw him was the day Léa died. He had just been sacked from the restaurant where he worked. He'd been informed that his appearance left a great deal to be desired and that some of their customers had complained about him, about his appearance and his strong smell of alcohol, sweat and tobacco.

Léa LIVED ON MY RIGHT. She was the landlord's daughter. She moved in one Sunday in November, two years to the day after I moved in. Every other evening, she had dinner three floors down, sharing in the parental boredom and watching a film directed by Claude Sautet or Yves Boisset on Channel Two. The first time I saw her, she was on the staircase carrying boxes, lugging them from the third to the sixth floor. Her long black hair framed her face, eyes like glass marbles, separated by a narrow, pointed nose. I offered to help and at first she glared at me. "I live upstairs," I told her, although that didn't seem to reassure her. Still, I picked up a box full of books and we made repeated trips up and down the stairs. Having set down the last box in the room lit by a bare bulb hanging from the recently glossed ceiling, we sat on the floor and she unpacked a seven-branched candelabrum, lit the candles and turned off the light. Her eyes quivered in the glow of the flames and we shared a bottle of port. I looked round and my attention was caught by a black and white face on the chest of drawers and the shelves, the face of a young girl who looked disturbingly like her.

"Who's that?"

"My grandmother. She died in Auschwitz."

I left her room around eight o'clock that evening, drunk and haunted by the intense gaze of her grandmother, that young woman with her hair drawn back and thin lips who seemed to be judging, appraising and absolving me from every corner of the room. How many times have I dreamt about that transparent, unreal woman stroking my cheek and hair, smiling at me before disappearing or suddenly wearing my own mother's face? There were also times when her face began to dissolve and turned into a horrific skeleton that was being pulverised, obliterated without a trace after being destroyed. I'd get out of bed shaking and, dripping with sweat, I'd go to the toilet on the corridor and throw up for ages.

Several days went by after our first meeting, I was working nights behind the reception desk in a hotel, she was spending her days at university in Paris and, although our rooms were next to each other, she might easily not have existed, not have moved in there, she might just have been a sallow, hazy apparition. It was her voice that woke me, one December evening. The sound of her breathing was coming through the wall, reaching my ears as if in a dream. I opened my eyes and her bed must have formed a continuation of mine, our hair divided by the thin plaster wall, head to head. She was moaning in a disturbingly childlike, heart-rending voice. The next day, in the corridor, I met some guy coming out of her room. He must have been at least fifty with a pot belly and tiny eyes.

The same thing happened many times. I didn't bump into her again for weeks and the only sign she was there could be heard in the evening. The men usually left a few hours after giving a deep groan that came through the wall. I'd get out of bed and open the door a crack. I'd watch them walk past and it was never the same man twice.

I didn't see Léa again until the end of winter. The months when Paris was only bearable at night, in the artificial warmth of the lights, reflected on car bonnets and the pavements glistening with rain, were coming to an end. She looked older that day. She was coming back home to pick up a few things as her parents were away for two days and she had planned to spend the night three floors down in that suite of rooms, their stifling, musty decor. I asked her if she would be on her own and she said, "Yes," with an odd smile, then added that I could visit her, if I liked. I should just ring at the tradesman's entrance around eight o'clock that evening.

She opened the door and her tired eyes were unreadable. Something seemed completely dead inside her and made you want to take her in your arms, kiss her forehead, watch over her through the night and nurse her better from some fever. I followed her into the profound silence of the living room; sitting at one end of the sofa she tucked her feet under her thighs and her knees stared at me. I filled two glasses with whisky and her face flickered gently in the candlelight. I don't remember exactly what we talked about that evening, all I remember is her gaze, her narrow nose, the taste of alcohol and the velvet of the armchairs, the black cotton of her dress, the line of mascara under her eyes. I had already drunk a great deal when I tried to kiss her. She pulled away gently, smiled at me and said: "You know there's someone else." I just asked:

"What about the others?"

"What others?"

"The others. The men you take to your room. The men I meet in the corridor."

"They've got nothing to do with it."

"What do you mean, they've got nothing to do with it?"

"I'm telling you, they've got nothing to do with it."

I didn't press the point. I filled our glasses, put an old vinyl record on the record player and asked her to dance. She stood up with a faint smile on her lips, a light in her eyes that told me I'd just scored a point, that she was pleased at my lack of reaction, that she was touched by my invitation to join me in the middle of the Persian rug. We lurched among the still lifes. The aristocratic pattern of the wallpaper spun endlessly, quivering in the flickering candlelight. She snuggled up to me, light and fragile, the bone of her shoulder blade was finer than a needle. My arms completely enveloped her and I felt as if any sudden movement might shatter her like crystal on marble. My eyes closed in the scent of her hair; hers had been closed for ages, the record played endlessly, stuck in a waltz time that was perfect for us. When I reopened my eyes, my shirt was damp with tears. I gently moved her body away from mine. I wiped her eyes with my fingertips, and I can still feel her mouth against mine, her surrender, as if it were yesterday. On the sofa, with her head on my shoulder, Léa fell asleep. We stayed like that for ages and I emptied the bottle of whisky. In the last glimmers of light from a dying candle, the final nocturne on a record of Chopin, I fell asleep as well.

When I woke she was gone and I was naked under the wool of a blanket in the half-light of the heavy, drawn curtains. I looked round, I didn't remember a thing. I coughed at length before I could say her name. I repeated it several times but no one replied. My head weighed eight tons. I heard keys turning in the front door of the flat, the noise of the locks. I gathered my things at top speed. Wrapped in my orange blanket, I walked to the kitchen. Just before I left the flat, I heard my landlord's voice raised in amazement at finding the place in such a mess on his return. In the corridor, I bumped into my Russian neighbour. He burst into peals of loud laughter when he saw me half-naked. I shut the door of my room, just as he was asking if I'd screwed the landlord or his daughter.

That day, I called the café and told them I was sick. My boss didn't say a word. He never said anything, he let me get away with murder because he said I reminded him of his son. I slept until the middle of the afternoon and the thought of Léa's face and body never left my mind for a second. When I woke up, I pressed my ear against the wall. I heard her voice. She wasn't alone. Some guy said a few words I didn't catch. Then there was the usual sound of his breathing getting louder and her soft cries. It didn't last long and when he came, I wept. I opened the door slightly and sat down on the carpet, looking through the gap. A few minutes later, a man of about forty walked by. I closed the door quietly. I remember sitting there for at least two hours, my head in my hands. The tap dripped. I didn't have the strength to stand up.

After that, Léa and I were an item. We didn't meet regularly or plan anything. She would sometimes bang on the wall and I always replied. I tried banging in my turn several times but there was never any answer. I spoke her name, I called out to her but she didn't respond.

When I received her signal, I'd leave my room and go to hers, the door would be ajar. Her grandmother stared down at me with all her eyes from the high point of her twenty years, her diaphanous beauty, her ignorance of her fate. Shame seemed to hold me in its gaze; I was overcome by the horrific nature of the world and its barbaric darkness. I couldn't tear my eyes away from her, she looked so much like Léa, despite the dated hairstyle and pre-war clothes. The shelves were covered with candles of all sizes and colours. I walked into her room and it was like going into a chapel. With the curtains closed in the middle of the day, the room was bathed in an orange light. I sat on the bed and Léa sat facing me, cross-legged on the rug, lifting a cup of steaming tea to her lips. On her desk there were piles of law books and Hebrew books, incense burning and a black cat asleep. She would let it out and I had almost trampled it on the stairs or in the gloom of the corridor. It meowed timidly and had got into the habit of defecating in front of my door. I would have liked to open its head and take out every single image of Léa it kept there. Her face bent over dull French law, her eyes closed when she slept, her head nodding gently when listening to music, her lips framing mysterious words, prayers, canticles, her mouth sighing when she fucked.

We had our habits. As the day drew to a close, she would play records one after the other, Yiddish, Hungarian or Gypsy chants that we listened to reverently, leaning against her bed, our legs stretched out on the Indian rug. At times, her mouth froze in an enigmatic grin. Afterwards she'd turn down the volume and ask me how far I'd got. I'd either tell her about the chapter I'd just written, or I'd talk about my procrastination and the problems I was having. I'd also keep her up to date with approaches I'd made to Parisian publishers. She enthused about every episode, every formal brainwave, the slightest word of encouragement I might have received from the lowliest trainee with nothing better to do. Later in the evening, after two or three glasses of red wine, we'd make love. It was often very fast, rough and brutal, other times very slow and tender, but afterwards we always stayed in each other's arms for ages and I caressed her eyes while she cried for no apparent reason. As the weeks went by, her body acquired countless marks, bruises, small scars, although I had no idea what had caused them. I comforted her without knowing what for and she did the same. It felt as if we were a mildly incestuous brother and sister, lost and bewildered in this dark world, wide-eyed and terrified as we gazed at frozen regions where nothing more could be done. We shivered with cold inches from the radiator.

All this time, I still often heard her moaning through the wall. As the days went by, her cries became terser, more distressing. The door would slam a few minutes later and on several occasions I heard her scream: "Get out, get the fuck out of here". Right to the end, I never knew why she fucked those men, what she was trying to achieve by offering herself up like that. All I knew about her was what she chose to tell me in her room with the flickering shadows, that tomb, that open burial chamber. Between the drawn curtains, we could see clouds and treetops, sometimes we could see for miles, everything was clear-cut and sharp, but usually it was just Paris and its slate roofs. As the weeks went by, the flat filled up with fabrics, dark velvet, heavy materials, thick books, candles, paintings. We sometimes spent the whole day in there without realising, we went to ground as if we were caught in an everlasting winter. Léa never talked about her parents, she turned the conversation back to her grandmother, to Auschwitz, to Budapest, where she lived for a year; she was just a child and didn't remember anything about it. I listened to her and her voice was heartbreaking. It was the voice of a world-weary little girl.

We did go out sometimes, the way you come up for air when you're underwater. She'd choose our route and I'd follow her. We walked through Paris, wrapped in darkness. We were cold and the Seine was calm. The Île Saint-Louis and the Marais were her favourite haunts, as well as the Jardin du Luxembourg, where I liked to doze, my face turned to the sun by the edge of the lawns or the ornamental lake, or in the shade of the fountain. She took me to cinemas where they showed foreign films I'd never even heard of, most of them extremely sad, wonderfully long, melancholy and full of despair. From time to time, she'd enter a café and introduce me to a female friend. I'd stay with them for a few minutes then make myself scarce. That's how I met Claire.

It was also around that time that I'd sometimes see my mother. I mean, really see her. The café was occasionally empty and she'd hurry by in the reflection of a window. I'd abandon the glasses I was rinsing and say to my boss, "I'm going out," in a tone that required no answer. "What's up? You look like you've seen a ghost." Out in the street, she was no more than a distant silhouette, a back covered in the black cotton of a coat, a cascade of long blonde hair. I followed her from a distance. She walked down the Rue du Pont-Neuf or the Rue de Rivoli, crossed the Seine heading towards Saint-Germain-des-Prés or took the Rue des Pyramides to the Opéra district. I caught up with her at the red lights. She sensed me on her heels, turned round and every time it was a new face, differing only slightly from my mother's. Every time, a small detail set them apart, small enough to create confusion, but obvious enough to remove any shadow of a doubt there and then. It does no good telling myself that her death should have been enough to dissuade me from following strangers whom I thought were her.

Paris was flooded with hallucinations, fleeting apparitions at the corner of a street, in the shade of a porch, the reflection of a window. Paris was overflowing with doubles of my mother. Thin, blonde women, pale and unassuming, hurrying along the pavement, between cars, disappearing into metro entrances, the lobby of a hotel, the coded door of a town house. Strangely these women were nearly always elegant and mysterious. I'd hear their heels clicking beneath the arcades of the Louvre, I'd walk in the footprints made by their steps in the sand of the Tuileries, unable to take my eyes from their shadow on the cobblestones of the Place Saint-Sulpice, in the coolness of the fountains in summer. I'd sit near them in the cinemas of Montparnasse, brush their hands, their wrists, on the stalls of second-hand booksellers on the quai des Grands Augustins. I'd stare at their backs on café terraces as they sipped smoked teas, Martinis or glasses of Pouilly on the Boulevard Saint-Germain, Rue de Buci, Rue de Seine or Place de l'Odéon. I'd breathe in their perfume on the elevated railway between Anvers and Belleville, where they would get off and head for a shabby building on the Rue Julien Lacroix, not far from the park overlooking the entire city, where the sky stretched away as far as the eye could see.

I'd also meet them at the reception desk of the hotel where I worked as a nightwatchman on the Rue de la Lune, on the fringes of the Strasbourg-Saint-Denis district. They would arrive around midnight with their black coats, scarves and glossy black leather handbags.

Tall, taciturn, invariably sleazy characters would come in before them, blocking my view as they turned their backs on me and lit a cigarette while I handed over the key to a comfortless room in exchange for a banknote. They would start climbing the stairs and I still hadn't seen their face. Pouring myself more coffee, heart racing, I'd wonder what my mother was doing with these men, I'd imagine her secret life. In the middle of the night, they would come back down, slip on their court shoes in front of my desk and, lifting their head, would smile at me. Naturally, none of them were my mother, and how could they have been. The night had never seemed to pass so slowly before. I'd sit there dozing, glancing occasionally at the tiny television, on which animals were shaking themselves and snorting. Sometimes I made notes, drafted a chapter, but I always remained in a trance, a sort of waking dream in which I'd thought I'd seen my mother, in which I'd imagined quite irrationally that she might be alive and turn up one night in a shabby hotel on a lover's arm.

One day in March, I saw her again and she was ahead of me on the path in the parc Monceau. A long red coat hung to her calves, similar to the one she was wearing so many years ago when she crossed another park and we waited for her in the car near the gates. Several times she stopped to look at a tree, a merry-go-round, a flower bed, two well-behaved children in navy-blue outfits. I drew closer and her perfume was the same, her coat threadbare as if she'd been wearing it constantly for nearly fifteen years now. A golden light was caressing the manicured lawns, spring was in the air in Paris and my heart was in my mouth. She swept into the metro and we found ourselves face to face in the carriage rattling towards porte Dauphine. In the rush-hour crowds, our faces almost touching, I accidentally brushed her hand. She gave me a sad smile to show there was no harm done. Naturally she was a little older, but it was her, or at least I convinced myself it was. A star of small wrinkles radiated from the outer edges of her eyes. Her mouth sagged slightly at the corners. She was still just as thin, almost transparent, but she had a new-found aura of serenity, an air of relaxation. My head was buzzing, the blood was pounding in my temples and my legs had turned to water. My brain was a jumble of thoughts, I couldn't think clearly any more, but one thing was plain: I was standing face to face with my mother. She hadn't recognised me, but then how could she, I was only a little boy when she'd made her escape from that hotel; it was the middle of the night and she'd vanished into the sleeping town, while another woman fell from the cliffs. In the morning, in the overheated carriage of a regional train, she'd watched the fields rush by in the rain, while in Étretat they were fishing an unrecognisable, broken body from the water. What mystery woman had we mourned all those years? What stranger had we buried six feet down in an anonymous cemetery in a suburb of Paris?

We got off at Victor Hugo. Evening was falling on the chubby, light-gold blocks of flats, tall windows hung with net curtains, tree-lined avenues on which there wasn't a soul to be seen. Sparkling, virtually new cars were parked along the curb. She walked into a bar, sat down near the window half-hidden by little burgundy velvet curtains. Like me, she smoked Cravens and ducked her head as she put her cigarette between her lips. She was probably waiting for someone but no one turned up. She kept checking her watch and she wore black gloves on her hands. It was eight o'clock when she stood up and I watched her red figure walk away in the suddenly dark evening. At twenty-six Rue Longchamp, she keyed in a code, then disappeared.

Two days later, I went back to that address. I scanned the windows. The building looked uninhabited, as did the street, the district. Trees scratched against the facades, I waited for hours and everything seemed suspended. Eventually she appeared. It had to be my mother walking towards me, I was sure of it. She entered the building and I followed her. The staircases were wide and carpeted with a long royal-blue runner. A wrought-iron gate opened into a lift panelled with varnished wood. Our faces were superimposed in the mirror and my lips silently pronounced the word "Mum". "Sorry, were you talking to me?" That voice, I thought I'd forgotten it, but it suddenly flooded back, familiar and intact. We got out at the fourth-floor landing. She turned the keys in the lock and asked: "Are you a friend of Louis's?" I said I was and she showed me into a vast, unfurnished flat. "He shouldn't be long. Would you like some coffee?" A sofa draped with a sheet stood in the empty living room. The large windows overlooked the street and identical blocks of flats. There were papers, letters and envelopes scattered about on the parquet floor. A telephone rang in another room. I heard footsteps in the corridor and her voice saying a few words. She hung up the receiver and rejoined me; she was holding a tray with two tinkling cups and she hadn't taken off her gloves. "He's not coming today. Something's come up. You can come back tomorrow, if you like." We drank our coffee and, when one of us said something, our voices echoed strangely in the huge room. I reminded her of someone but she didn't say who. She again told me to come back the next day, when Louis would be there. I left the flat and the words I hadn't spoken made my lips burn.

I'M COLD AND THE SKY IS A LITTLE BRIGHTER. Freighters pass each other in the distance. On the rusty decks my brother sails by endlessly, perhaps forever. I don't know whether I miss him. I think he belongs to another life and that, since my mother's death, I've learnt to accept what happens, not to fight anything any more. When it comes down to it, I think the hole she made inside me was already so big and deep that when he disappeared into it he couldn't have made it any larger.

I don't know *precisely* when my brother made his first appearance in my honeycombed memory; when, exactly, he emerged from those sands with a recognisable face, voice, figure. I think he becomes confused with me or my mother at times between the ages of eight and eleven. Surprisingly, though, it seems as if I've known him for much longer than that. I don't think that the things I've forgotten about him are important or are buried so deep. They are still there, on the tip of my tongue, so to speak.

From Les Abbesses to Marseilles, from his escape to his disappearance, I only saw him sporadically, only talked to him on the phone maybe some fifteen times. Antoine said very little about the countries he visited, listed his stopovers, told me when he was coming and that was about it. If he had time, he came to Paris and knocked on my door. That was five or ten years ago and Antoine has never seen Chloé, has never been told about her birth. It was five or ten years ago, maybe more, I've lost track of time over the years. Once a year, Antoine would scrape at my door saying: "It's me." He'd come in and hug me, remark that my room was almost as small as his cabin and help himself to a beer. He'd turn on the television, we'd watch some crap, smoking joints that he'd roll one after the other. When it was dark, we'd walk alongside the deserted park, past Batignolles, reaching the Place de Clichy, flashing like a merry-go-round in the red night. We'd go into the bars, where my brother invariably ended up in the arms of a girl dressed in black, with painted lips, dyed hair and an exposed cleavage, and I'd make myself scarce, I'd go home completely drunk, collapse on the bed and he'd wake me up a few hours later. He'd collapse on the couch and bang his head against the sloping ceiling. He'd ask me to open the window even in winter, he'd want to breathe in the smell of the sea. I did as he asked and we'd be so cold. We'd fall asleep beneath three blankets, side by side in the icy room, the radiators turned off at night by the landlord. Antoine would be wasted, he'd smoked, taken Ecstasy, snorted a line of coke, he'd talk in his sleep, choke back his tears and chew his lips noisily, he'd shake and start shouting for no reason. The woman down the corridor would hammer on the door, yell at us to shut up, and my brother would sob even harder, and I think that deep down this was the only way we could talk about mum's death. The only way we ever managed to talk about it was by snuffling against each other's faces, letting our tears mingle and holding each other tight in the wintry darkness.

Nothing gets to me now. Nothing, except Claire and Chloé. And tonight, I'm not going to talk about them. No. Or at least not really. No, I'm not going to say anything about them, perhaps because I'm superstitious, yes, probably, to keep them safe from misfortune, ward off the evil eye. I'll talk about them another day, another night, and then I'll describe my daughter's laughter and her hair against my cheek, and I'll describe Claire's expression and my head buried between her breasts, her fair-minded, straightforward remarks that make me walk with my head held up high, the tenderness that keeps us together, the comfort of living by her side.

The sky is lighter and tinges of pink, yellow and blue are breaking through the clouds. I leave my rocky shelter, dawn is slowly breaking and the sea is lapping around the white, perpendicular stone. I lean over the edge, it's no longer so dark and soon it's a pale bluish-grey caressed by a horizontal sun. I walk towards the beach, the earth is slippery and my steps leave footprints. Somebody's watching me, there's somebody behind me, I turn and there's no one there, just the veil left by an absence, a shadow withdrawing. Like the hole my mother left in my stomach, like the hole that is my childhood. A footprint, a gap, barely more, barely enough to believe that there was something rather than nothing there.

By the time I reach the foot of the steps, day has broken, pale and sparkling. An old man is walking on the shingle, he stares at the emerging cliffs that look yellowish at this hour. On the terraces, men are carrying chairs, wiping tables pearled with drops of water. A few dormer windows glint at the front of hotels. I shiver, numb with the desire to sleep. A fat woman on reception looks suspiciously at me, I nod hello. The room is still dark, curtains drawn against the brightening light. Claire is fast asleep and Chloé, sitting beside her, looks up at me, says, "Papa," then asks: "Where were you?" I'm overwhelmed, seeing her like this. I hug her tightly, whisper in her ear that I love her, that Papa went for a walk, went to watch the birds, that she mustn't be worried, ever, that I'll always be there for her. She gives me a wet kiss on the lips and asks to watch cartoons. I turn on the television, leave the volume control turned to the lowest setting, take off my jacket and slip between her and her mother. I'm tired, my feet are like blocks of ice. Claire takes my hand and murmurs: "You're freezing," before going back to sleep.

THE MONTH BEFORE HER DEATH, Léa only banged on the wall of her room a handful of times. I'd go in and she'd barely look up to greet me. She would light scores of candles and even at night did her best to make sure none of them went out. She was very quiet, even contemplative, and her eyes seemed to dominate her face. On the last two occasions, her room smelt of ether and on her desk, beside a small glass of water, there were a few pills left in various aluminium blister packs. (I don't know how she managed to get her hands on so many drugs, which she mixed according to her needs. Perhaps one of her family was a pretty liberal doctor. Or perhaps it was one of her 'lovers'?) We made love and there was a steely, faraway look in her eyes as I moved back and forth inside her. Distraught, disturbing expressions crossed her face, revealing a deep absence, a distancing. We fucked in silence and afterwards I hugged her, twice, hard enough to smother her, as if that might save her, the way the living hold their dead in their arms just before they take their last breath. I held her tight and her body was cold and stiff. I didn't know it then but she was already far away, and nothing could bring her back to the surface.

Even now, when I think back to our last hours curled up against each other, like two children hiding, trembling with cold, fear and misery, I still remember the precise feel of her body suddenly harder than wood, its lifeless texture, her corpse-like expression. I don't want to think about what one day finally pushed her over, when she was teetering on the edge, like many of us, like me. I don't want to think about that or her worrying resemblance to Lorette in those last days, their fissured faces, deserted by blood, by life and the world's pulse, or about my mother, about their similar, deliberate deaths, their distress and their selfishness, the way they denied that I might be able to secure them to the world, keep them here, *make a difference*. All it proves is that none of them were really *attached* to me, when I would have spent my life being attached to others, hanging on for dear life, even when they were nothing but soapy boards, shaky crews, unreliable, unsteady associates. And if all there is to life is this slender thread linking us together, there's no doubt that mine was defective, flimsy and slippery, as if eroded by salt.

The day she died I couldn't hear anything when I pressed my ear to the wall except the sound of water gushing. A puddle had formed outside her door in the corridor, spreading over the tiles. The floor in her room was sodden, the curtains were drawn, and about a hundred lit candles flickered. On the walls, her grandmother smiled shyly from countless copies of the same photo. I pushed open the bathroom door and she was lying in the bath, waxen in her flowery dress bloated with water, her skin and lungs flooded. I turned off the taps and rushed out. My fat Russian neighbour was standing in the doorway, his skin sallow and his eyes glazed. I have no idea what the hell he was doing there. He looked questioningly at me.

"She's dead. She's killed herself."

That's all I could say. He crossed the room, went into the bathroom in his turn, as if he wanted to check I wasn't lying. He came out again and his legs seemed to give way under his massive body. He slumped into the armchair and didn't get up again, muttering incomprehensible words.

I went back into the bathroom. I lifted Léa out of the narrow bath. Her body was wet and icy, like a fish. In the room, on the bed, dressed in mauve and covered in tiny pink flowers, Léa was still dead. The door opened and it was her father. He came in and the fabric of his charcoal suit flapped around his skinny legs. He didn't look at us, we were invisible or non-existent, he saw his daughter and collapsed. We stayed quiet for a moment, waiting, then suddenly it felt as if the air were freezing around us, turning our blood to pale blue ice. After a long while, he stood up and, in a very calm voice, ordered us to get out. We could both vacate our flats, he never wanted to see us again, he gave us ten days to clear off. We left the room in silence.

THE FUNERAL WAS TWO DAYS LATER. I didn't empty my flat before I left. I just filled a bag. I only took the bare essentials. A few clothes, my papers, my manuscripts, my notebooks. I left the key in the door and I didn't have a spare. I joined the funeral cortège on a path in the Montmartre Cemetery. The men were all very tall and bald and wore long cashmere coats; the women were in dark suits with designer sunglasses. The trees soared like arrows into the perfectly blue sky. I remained in the background. Someone put a hand on my shoulder. It was Claire and we fell into each other's arms, among the tombs where frozen birds were nesting. I asked her if she wanted to go any closer. She answered that she couldn't, that she wouldn't be able to bear the sight of the hole, the coffin, the earth on top. We went for a coffee in a café on the Place de Clichy. It was getting dark and we were still there. We were drunk and unhappy. That evening, I didn't let anyone know, I didn't go to work serving at the bar. I didn't go the next day either. And then I never went again. I thought my boss would understand. I didn't go back to the hotel either.

We left the café, and all around us the Place de Clichy revolved like a merry-go-round, a fairyland of neon lights and headlamps. We walked to her place. She was already living in that gloomy flat with its crooked walls, the orangey-red floor tiles, the three windows opposite the tall, cracked walls, the rooms overlooking the courtyard. She didn't turn on the lights and the floor was swaying. We undressed and nothing could warm our icy bones, our frozen blood. We spent the night with our eyes open, motionless and entwined, under piles of blankets. In the silence of the building, broken only occasionally by the sound of water trickling through the pipes, the distant ringing of an alarm clock, I felt her tears on my shoulder, against my cheek and in my mouth. I woke up around midday and she was curled in a ball on the couch, very pale in the morning light, a ray of sunshine brightening her hair and warming her reddened skin. I haven't let her out of my sight since.

SPENDING ALL THOSE YEARS lurking in that room at the end of a narrow corridor, hiding myself away so that I'd never be found by my father or anyone else, was a little like living in a nursing home. A long stay without any doctors or any other medication than alcohol. There were rooms, my neighbours were inmates and our paths would sometimes cross. We went out from time to time but we always came back. Two years later, I was rushed home to France from Lisbon as a matter of urgency. I spent several weeks in an arcade of wards surrounded by a park with bare trees and frost-covered benches, and it wasn't all that different when I think about it.

I don't know what made Claire think of Lisbon, perhaps Pessoa. The publication of my second novel, which was greeted by a wall of silence, kept my head below water, and I think she felt it was a sort of last-ditch trip. Spring was in the air and we had rented a room on the banks of the Tagus. I drank all night and all day and I never went out without two or three reserve bottles in the big pockets of a voluminous raincoat. We went walking through the streets, I was half drunk and she was exhausted from supporting me. Steep flights of steps led down into narrow lanes where everything had a neglected air. Claire held my hand, I was drunk and it was as if I were possessed, lucid and mad. Everything suddenly seemed so clear and bright, perhaps too much so, as if I were being dazzled or having an epiphany or a dizzy turn accentuated by the alcohol and the drugs. I raced down the streets singing, I sat on the steps, ran my hand over the smooth, dusty surface of the azulejos. I laughed for no reason, ran towards the river, looked up at the dazzling sky. Claire looked at me oddly but without any anger or reproach, occasionally she whispered that I was acting like a madman and I told her that the town was my mind, that I was a crazy mind in a crazy town. I really was on the verge of madness, swinging between bouts of exultation and dejection that had never reached such proportions. Lisbon served as a mirror, a state of slow deterioration. Like the town, I surrendered to exhaustion, I gave up, let myself go, laughed when I wanted to laugh, cried the same way and screamed in the night. Claire smiled affectionately at me when I talked to her about leaving. Other times, gazing at me as I sat drinking beneath a tree, she couldn't quite hold back her tears and I didn't care. We ate in bistros where regulars chewed pieces of cod swimming in oil in front of the television. We got back late and I collapsed on the bed, the beams spinning on the ceiling. I was crumbling and everything around me seemed out of kilter. Claire took care of me, undressed me as she'd done so many times in Paris, made me throw up in the toilet when necessary. She performed all these services with so much gentleness and so little pride, that I hated her, I showered her with insults and she cried. Her face was red and swollen with tears, I twisted her wrists and she fought back. Several times I slapped her. She scratched me, bit me and her nails gauged red scars into my skin. Several evenings in a row we fell asleep like this, no breath left for crying and screaming. The morning didn't bring a fresh start. We just picked up where we'd left off, slightly more hostile than the morning before, and I watched Claire slowly getting out of her depth. As for me, I can't describe the strange ferment of thoughts that filled my mind to bursting, the images that haunted me. Everything was a wasteland and nothing made any sense or had any point. Anxiety attacks followed flashes of lucidity, moments of blinding clarity preceded states of fear. I was experiencing unrelenting paranoia attacks, suffering from a kind of persecution complex, and I took it all out on Claire who stood it, stoical, patient, and grief-stricken. The floodgates opened and it seemed as if everything that had been waiting to explode was now erupting, as if everything that should have destroyed me was now doing so at top speed. I was consuming myself from the inside, my mind was disintegrating, the dykes were collapsing, I was at breaking point. The last evening we came back and I started threatening to commit suicide, I don't remember why. I heaped insults on Claire, screamed that she didn't love me, that she wanted to destroy me and humiliate me, that I'd had enough of her saintly expression, her nauseating kindness, that deep down all she felt for me was pity and that she made me sick. Then things got out of hand, I don't remember very much, except storming out, talking about dying. I was grinding my teeth, clenching my fists as I strode down flights of steps, streets, avenues. I walked through the night, wearing nothing but boxer shorts and a T-shirt, I had the distinct feeling that I was turning to dust, crumbling like a flaking wall, I had the distinct feeling that I was under threat, I was sure that Claire was following me and that she wanted to kill me slowly, suffocate me, eliminate me, snuff me out. After that, I don't remember anything. I woke up in a hospital and I was terribly hot. Claire was holding my hand and my mind was completely empty and unresponsive. My body was packed with cotton wool, my head with a light fog or an extremely thin tulle. I slept in the plane. Every hour, Claire made me swallow medication that knocked me out. I spent three months in a centre where they forced me to stop drinking. I didn't even notice the first two months go by. After that, what I mainly remember is the quiet, peaceful room, the park bathed in light, Claire holding my arm and kissing my neck, the odd pieces of news she brought from the outside world. The psychiatrist was a tall man with grey hair, he reminded me of the doctor I took Lorette to see, he talked to me in simple terms, took time to listen to me and was gentle in his manner with all the patients. I quietly did what he told me to do, I didn't drink and endured the weeks of dizziness, anxiety attacks and violent headaches that this involved. I simply bided my time and formed only very superficial relationships with the other patients, mixing very little, as I was frightened by their distress, I was afraid it would contaminate me. The therapist thought these were positive reactions. He said they proved my desire to be cured, that I was also superstitiously trying to break the unhealthy circle, to escape from unhappiness and dependence. I don't know. I have no idea whether he was right. After all, I had no control over my thoughts and he was only interpreting my behaviour. I think it was more that every single face reminded me of someone, made me think of friends or family. The two by the tree, the man in a tracksuit with nervous gestures he can't control, the very thin woman in a black dress, are Nicolas and Lorette. And that woman in the distance, always silently staring into space, occasionally visited by a man and two children, who try to no avail to coax a word, gesture or smile out of her, isn't that my mother? Isn't she going to be released one day, go with them to the seaside and at night leave the room, climb through the darkness towards the sky and the wind-blown fields, throw herself into the sea and die, her lungs filled with seaweed and sand?

I came out and it was summer. Paris was deserted. Claire had taken some holiday and I covered her lovely face with kisses. I would have liked to tell her that she had saved me, that every day she saved me, but I didn't say anything. A few days later, I emptied my first bottle of whisky. The medication kept me afloat, my nights were filled with nightmares and everything around me seemed swamped with sadness. I wrote obscure stories about alcoholic boxers, undertaker's assistants bending beneath the interminable weight of the dead. We left for Brittany a few months later.

After our unexpected meeting in that PMU bar on the Grands Boulevards, I never bumped into my father again. He vanished from my life and not once during all those years did I consider seeing him again or was tempted to find out how he was getting on. It was Claire who one day persuaded me to pick up the phone. Nine years had gone by without a word, without even a letter or postcard. I had published books, a film was in the pipeline and from time to time I was on the radio or my photo had appeared in magazines. I couldn't help thinking that maybe he'd hear me, come across my face somewhere and, why not, pop into the library to ask if they had his son's latest novel. But I never wondered for a second whether he was still alive. I don't know why, it just never crossed my mind, I couldn't imagine my father dead. Chloé had just been born. Claire insisted I tell my father, so he would at least know he was a grandfather. She thought that was the very least I could do and it would give me the chance to get back in touch. I looked at the phone hundreds of times, unable to pick up the receiver, breathing deeply to calm myself and find the strength and stupidity to call him, hear his voice, again, when it felt as if I were still running away from it and always would be, when it seemed sometimes that this was the hidden meaning of my life, to run away from my father and search endlessly for my runaway mother.

I don't remember what made up my mind, why on that particular day, maybe it was the evening, I'd probably been drinking, I found the strength, the courage to do it. I stood in the corridor, I could hear the radio in the sitting room and my daughter grizzling, a hungry creature with eyes closed and mouth wide open, searching for Claire's breast. Bird calls, noises from the gutters and the bowed trees reached me from outside. It rang once and I was ready to hang up as soon as I heard his voice. But that time, and every other time, the phone rang in the emptiness and no message, answering machine or voice interrupted that regular, synthetic pulse. Claire eventually convinced me that something had happened, that my father might be in hospital or maybe he'd moved and I pictured him in one of those old people's homes where gaunt, wild-eyed old men doze in the common room in front of the television, crap themselves while they're asleep, receive visits from nephews whose name they can't remember and endure the constant presence of nurses and auxiliaries who speak to them in a tone generally reserved for small children or animals. Places smelling of bleach where bodies continually fail, sag and suffer, where life withers, flesh decays, stinking of death and mildew, like the odour of skin when a plaster cast is removed after months of immobility. Places where the mind remains vigilant but the mouth becomes as unresponsive as the legs or sphincter. I pictured my father shut away in this world of the living dead, I pictured his anger taking other forms, coming up against other walls, other faces, other gestures, I pictured him as one of those insufferable, spiteful, quick-tempered, dreadful old men, who are the bane of nurses. I pictured him like that and still I dialled his number several times a day. Once or twice I tried my luck in one of the local hospitals but no, his name wasn't on any of the admission registers, the secretaries on the phone asked me if I was his son and I said yes and they always wondered out loud: how come he doesn't know where his own father is, if he's ill and what he's suffering from? I didn't listen to their tirades, I hung up and signalled to Claire that no, no one had seen him there either. She seemed more worried than I was. Despite what I'd been able to tell her about my relationship with him, she always ended the conversation in the same way, with this irrefutable phrase: "But he is your father." I've never understood what people meant by that, what made family ties so different from other ties that they couldn't be broken even when everything pointed to that, even when they made us feel too insecure or trapped. In the end I gave in. One November day we caught the train in Brest and when we got to Paris, everything was damp and foggy, wreathed in the filthy grey of towns, sodden with sticky sadness. We took the RER. Wrapped in a large blanket, Chloé was sleeping and grunting, fidgeting and wiggling her fingers, clutching at my nose and ears. We passed rows of blocks of flats and windows, warehouses, industrial estates and retail parks, lines of houses identical to the one where I grew up and where I was going to see my father again. Ten minutes before the stop, you could already glimpse the towers in the estate, those eight pearl-grey towers that, at certain times of the day, plunged our house and garden into shadow. From Lorette's room, we could monitor the old man's comings and goings, watch out for him to leave, then reoccupy the place, return to our rooms or watch television in the living room. Chloé woke up when the train slowed down and we had to wait on a bench on the deserted platform, beneath a plum-coloured roof, while it drizzled and my daughter sucked at Claire's breast. They were both hidden behind a pale blue blanket and a song by Joe Dassin, 'Salut les amoureux' I think, was being piped through the speakers.

Nothing had changed of course. The Mammouth sign had been replaced by the red lettering of the Auchan brand name, the car park had been extended, the towers had been repainted and, at their base, between two rows of cars covered in graffiti, a building had been constructed to house a *Maison de Quartier*, adjacent to a square of cement surrounded by wire fencing with a basketball goal at either end. With

Chloé snuggled against my stomach, my nose buried in her fine hair, breathing in her smell of sleep, soap and curdled milk, I walked along intact, fossilised streets deserted for so many years, where only the makes of cars, their models and the colour of their paintwork, had changed over time. This world made no sense at all, but then it really never had.

The cramped house stood in the middle of the remodelled garden. Cement had been laid where there used to be tall grass, a close-cropped lawn grew around the foot of a young cherry tree, orderly rows of flowers were planted along the path. The walls were roughcast and hidden by laurel trees, bamboos and ivy. The iron gate had been repainted and locked. I rang the doorbell. A woman came out of the house and walked towards us. She must have been around fifty, maybe more, and her sparrow-like face was framed by dyed, permed hair. She looked fearful, the way people always look when they're approached by a stranger, as if the world were populated only by cut-throats and child rapists, as if the world really did resemble the poor fiction offered up by the television news. She asked us what we wanted by jutting out her chin. "I'm looking for my father," I heard myself say, while Chloé rubbed her face against my skin.

"Your father?"

"Yes, my father. He lives here."

"Here? I should be surprised if he did. Unless my husband has children and has never told me."

I looked at Claire and we weren't thinking the same thing. Claire was already picturing my father in an old people's home, in long-stay hospital care or dead. As for me, fleeting images were inadvertently running through my mind, in which my father had remarried without telling anyone about us, my mother, Antoine and me, had started over with a clean slate, silently crossing out our names, beginning a life washed clean of the three of us, leaving his memory as good as new, unburdened by that former, oppressive life he never loved, the way he never loved Antoine and me, or at least as far as I knew, and anyway of course I knew nothing about it, since everything was buried deep in the sands of memory and the harder I dug, the deeper I sank. Chloé started crying and it was incredible how intuitive she was and how she could sense all my feelings. I couldn't speak. I would have liked to say that I couldn't care less about the house abandoned by my father and with him everything that had happened before, the last memories of my mother roaming through this dreary house, I would have liked to tell myself that in my heart of hearts I didn't give a damn about this place, the altered garden, the same street and what that brought back, the smells, the light, the texture of the air, the cement under my feet and the towers in the distance, I would have liked to say that I didn't feel a thing, that being here after so many years left me cold but it wasn't true and my eyes clouded and there was a knot in my throat, mum was walking in the garden, barefoot in the damp grass, and Antoine was watching me, his face bathed in sunshine, his right eye screwed shut because of the light. Everything was reduced to blurred shapes, misty glimpses. Claire's voice reached me as if through fleece or cotton wool, faraway as in a dream. She was chatting to the woman, she'd been there for two years now, she didn't even know his name, we ought to ask the neighbours, they might know, she was sorry, she couldn't help us, goodbye. I followed Claire as if in a trance, I saw the woman next door come out of her house, wipe her hands on her apron, I recognised her, she used to yell at us when we kicked the ball into her garden because of her flowers. I heard what she said when she talked about my father, his illness and the day the ambulance came for him, the countless times she visited him at the hospital and, poor man, she was the only one who came, his children had abandoned him, isn't loneliness a terrible thing these days, people are buried with no one there, dying when their children don't give a damn. I remember thinking vaguely that it was the parents' job to look after their children and not the other way round, I hugged Chloé close and that thought became even stronger, I thought about protecting her for her whole life, I thought about seeing to it that she never went short of anything, not only food, money or a roof over her head, but also kisses, affectionate gestures and words of endearment, I thought: 'When I'm old, I'll stay out of the way, and my whole life through, Chloé, I'll stay out of your way, discreet but always there, I'll be there only if you want me there, if you need me there, if you think it'll help.' She said: "It's too late now," and glared at me with the eyes of an old magpie, the eyes of an old woman who yells at children when they play in the street, when their balls land on her flowers, she said that and also that he was dead and buried, and that she had visited him in the hospital right up to the bitter end. She added, shooting me a sideways look, that she wondered what could have kept children so busy that they neglected their own father, particularly when he was living on his own, and didn't even know he'd died of cancer. She carried on talking about him, how thin he'd become at the end, how he used to call the nurses and doctors by the first names of his two children, Antoine and Olivier, how he kept saying "my darling" to a slim, blonde auxiliary nurse whom he thought was his wife, and it's true she did look like her. She talked about the meals she cooked for him all that time, after the second son left—she said that as if I weren't there, as if I weren't the son in question, she spoke about me in the third person when we were standing opposite each other—and she came to do his housework once a week and the poor man was all on his own, yet so kind, chatty, witty, never raised his voice, never spoke a word out of place, always very polite and never complained, even when he was in so much pain from the cancer, which made him lose his hair and his reason. Then she spoke about the cemetery, the funeral which only she and a colleague from the time when he was a taxi driver attended, along with two or three brothers and sisters who had spent the time listing their grievances, countless petty reproaches which made it apparent that they simply didn't like him. Why is it that everyone who got to know my father hated him, and that the only person who might once have loved him had preferred to throw herself from the top of a cliff?

Chloé slobbered on my shirt, her warm, damp body against my torso, her wet, toothless mouth chewing the finger I gave her to bite or the collar of my coat. We walked through the grey streets and Claire squeezed my fingers in her gloved hand. She turned to look at me, watching my face for a reaction, and I couldn't believe it, I couldn't come to terms with the fact that he was dead or work out if that made any difference to me either way. I didn't know if he'd taken something of my mother with him to the grave and I think that was the only thing that mattered to me. What had he taken of her when so much had already been stolen from me? What had he taken of me, of my memory, of the impenetrable sands of my childhood? Had all those years disappeared for good this time, buried six feet under, pressed up against him in the darkness of the coffin? We turned our backs on the trunk road. In the distance, behind the rows of houses, we could see trees leaning over the river, and barges were sailing by in the gaps. High walls stained with water rose near the deserted sports ground, the dirty pinks, faded blues of terraces, walls spray-painted with huge swathes of graffiti, moth-eaten sports field, rusted goalposts without nets. The cemetery was tiny and sheltered from view, scattered with white or pale grey pebbles forming well-manicured paths. Claire pushed open the heavy iron gate. Chloé was hungry, she was fidgeting and crying in the silence that enveloped everything, strangely deadening the surrounding noise. My father's tombstone was at the back on the right, a stark slab, unadorned by flowers or anything. Claire sat on the cold stone; Chloé opened her mouth wide and sucked on her breast. At that moment, something seemed to make sense vaguely, although I wasn't really sure what it was, while, with one hand in my coat pocket and the other holding a cigarette, standing beneath the pale, perfectly blue sky, I gazed at the woman I loved feeding my daughter near my father's grave. We caught the train back that evening.

That night, it took me a long time to fall asleep. I spent several hours smoking by the window, then standing in the cramped wardrobe, among the clothes, my cheek pressed against the wall, which had become a habit of mine, although I didn't know why; it was as if I were still trying to hear Léa on the other side of the wall. Chloé was asleep next to her mother. I eventually dozed off around dawn, curled up on the couch in the living room. Through the half-open door I could hear their intermingled breathing, the little girl settled comfortably against the woman. I matched my breathing with theirs and all three of us were held in the same pattern of respiration at the heart of the cold, wind-blown house, filled with bunches of drying flowers and piles of books, records and magazines covered in dust. I fell into a deep sleep, a heavy, black darkness, as if submerged by dense, icy waters. And my father appeared, more real than in life. The forgotten father from when I was four, six then eight, the one I'd only seen in meaningless photos, that man with a moustache and pale, striped cotton shirts, busy in the garden and smiling, taking hold of my mother by the hips, or lifting Antoine towards the sky slashed by telegraph wires where little black birds sat in rows. I suddenly saw him, my father, with that sensation of intense lifelikeness you sometimes get in dreams. I heard his voice and felt his hand in my hair, his breath on my forehead as he carried me. The scenes scrolled past, sharper than memories, even more indisputable and unsettling. My father standing in front of a house I don't know, and behind him fields in the sunshine and mountains in the distance. Hands on hips he is watching us and we are perched in a tree. Antoine climbs down then it's my turn and my father holds out his arms, I let myself drop and he catches me and spins me round and the sun and his face whirl and blur, his face and his smile under the bright sun, then his voice in my ear, the harsh rasp of his cheek, the muscles of his sturdy arms. I'm six maybe seven and I hear his voice, for the first time I hear his voice and it's quiet and steady, sometimes cheerful, he calls me "my young pup", that's what he calls me and it's the first time, these words in his mouth, words like "my pup my poppet my pet". I follow him on my bike and we cross the bridge over a dead channel, we stop to watch the barges, the lighters, the buildings opposite, the planes overhead, which have just taken off or are about to land on the cement of Orly's runways. He turns to me and says: "Race you," and he lets me win. Further on, we play football and he catches me by the ankles and we sprawl in the grass and afterwards we drink sitting side by side out of breath, and he tells me the name of the trees and the birds. We're in the garden by the barbecue and mum shuts her eyes on the terrace and the sunshine gently nibbles her skin. I copy her and with our faces to the sun our eyelids turn orange. I open my eyes a crack and everything is hazy. I stretch out my fingers, I catch hold of a birch leaf, I hold it up to the sun and mum and I look at the world through it for hours. My father turns the hose on us and sprays us with water, mum screams and roars with laughter and Antoine arrives armed with bottles filled with water, he starts chasing my father who's laughing as hard as he can and I don't know how many times we run round the house like that and I don't recognise anything or anyone in these images, not my father or my mother, or my brother, not even me, and in my heart of hearts I don't know whether it was all just a dream, no truer than any other dream, just as illusory and unreal as if I'd dreamt that night I was fucking a famous actress or a girl from school, or about monsters from outer space, shut rooms, labyrinths, walking through the street in my pyjamas or bare feet or even, as I once did, about being a grown-up and a pupil in the fifth year surrounded by children.

After that, unlike my mother, my father deserted my dreams, just as he had deserted my life. After that, there were times when it seemed that something, part of my forgotten childhood, had become clearer, that a question had been answered, that when it came to knowing who my father was before my mother died, I had a reassuring response, and that my black hole was actually a well of tenderness, a platform for love. At other times, though, most of the time in fact, it felt as if the dream were just an illusion, nothing more, an invention, and anyway it didn't change anything, what we forget no longer exists. What fades from our minds also fades from our bodies, our blood, our life, leaving no trace, no mark, save for an empty space, a cold, dizzying drop.

I'm thirty-one and for a long time staying alive has been a full-time job, a plan, an objective. Maintaining a semblance of balance. Not falling to pieces or dissolving into tears. Not going under, allowing myself to be led astray by those who are now far away, to whom I was once attached and who weigh me down.

I'm thirty-one and it doesn't matter. I know how heavy the dead are. And I know about bad luck. I know about loss and devastation, the taste of blood, the wasted years and those that trickle through your fingers. I know how deep the sand is, I've experienced its resistance, its soft, ambiguous material. I know that nothing is dependable, that everything unravels, cracks and shatters, that everything withers and everything dies. Life damages the living and no one ever puts the pieces back together or picks them up.

Our lives are alike. Our lives are the same and troubled. Our memories are faded, eaten away by acid, full of holes like inferior cotton. Our future buried, our history unreadable, without frame or spinal column, all the lights off. Our lives are poorly assembled pieces, scattered bits that will never fit together. Our lives are modern and forgotten, tiny and discarded. Millions of lit windows on the façades, headlamps in the dark, bodies in the town.

Our lives are alike. Our lives are the same and lost. We've grown up in the shadow of cold, threatening fathers, the careworn frailty of our mothers, we hold each other close in frosted cities, identical, dreadfully silent houses, in streets sapped by anxiety and boredom, surrounded by dead adults. Yes, we've grown up in fear of our fathers, the troubled silence of our mothers, the empty space formed by abstract, imaginary places, without edge or centre. We weren't rich or poor, poor or rich, we believed in nothing and no one, and nothing and no one believed in us.

Our lives are alike. Our lives are the same and beyond recall. Our childhoods ooze boredom and fear, our teenage years shatter against invisible walls, our houses merge into one and are engulfed by the boundless landscape. And as time passes, we endlessly watch friends and family fall one by one, we see them disappear and die. Now we walk aimlessly and our feet scuff through ashes. We haven't experienced history. We have no idea where we're headed. We're not interested in the period, and society is a fiction too vast for us even to imagine. We're carried back and forth by the current and everything slips through our fingers. We hang on to what reassures us and holds on to us, links us together and, as a result, standing face to face with each other without ever touching, we don't feel so afraid and something finally seems to take shape. But nothing precise ever emerges anywhere, the wind is blowing and there's frost all around. One amongst many, we drift, trembling with cold we inch forward, like blind tadpoles. Everything gives way under our steps and in our hands life escapes like sand through our fingers. And yet we continue, most of us continue. We wipe the dust from our hands, from our knees. We dry the blood on our palms, we cross our fingers and we believe that by doing this we can keep misfortune at bay.

Our lives are alike. Our lives are the same and blighted. We mourn the same dead and live in the dark company of phantoms, our bodies become entangled and try in vain to find impossible comfort. Lost forever in the crowd, our lives fit into a thimble. And however tall we stand on tiptoe, we remain smaller than ourselves.

Our lives are alike. Our lives struggle, cry out in the night, scream and tremble with fear. We search for shelter forever. A place where the wind doesn't blow so hard. A place we can go. And that place of shelter is a face and that face is all we need.

Claire wakes and stretches, kisses me and Chloé throws herself at her, crowing with laughter. I go to sleep for a couple of hours. During that time, I'll hear their voices, their murmurs, their smothered laughter, the water running into the bath, the rustle of material. Later we'll go to the beach, throw stones into the grey and blue water. Then we'll walk high above the water and even later we'll drive home, towards other sands, other waters. There'll be hundreds of birds and the tide will be out. I already know that when I wake, when I open my eyes the curtains, everything will be still and radiant.

ACKNOWLEDGEMENTS

I would like to thank:

The county council of Seine-Saint-Denis for their help

My 'personal guard'
Julien Bouissoux, Alix Penent, Olivier Chaudenson

The 'readers over my shoulder'
Alain Raoust, Jean-Christophe Planche